Dogs of Essex

L.D.Blaney

Copyright © 2024 L.D.Blaney

All rights reserved.

ISBN: 9798304330725

To my daughter Iris whose resilience and intelligence inspire me every day.

Thank you
xx

6

CONTENTS

1   Hook   9

2   Link   20

3   The Well   31

4   Canis   45

5   Cerberus   52

6   Web   59

7   Mice   67

8   Wrong   75

9   The Music 82

10 The Piper 95

Part II HOOK

Lake Meadows, Billericay, United Kingdom - October, 2001.
'Thats manky Jace!'
'It is ent' it?!'
They gazed over the infected foot, his sock slipped off and rested on a small mound of mud near where they had nonchalantly placed their bait.
'And you say this was from stepping on a hook?'
His friend went cold reminiscing the event.
'Wandered into me mums shed barefoot and the fuckin' thing went right through me toe, should have gone A&E but I just put some numbing cream on it, downed some Vodi and pulled the fucker out-'
'And then?'
'Passed out din' I...mum fand me about five minutes later like a goldfish out of it's bowl, she bandaged it up and did her usual TCP game...I screamed like a right mug and then done...but now look!'
'Yeah, docs need lookin at that...'
They cracked open a couple of sneaky cans of lager and munched on petrol station pork pies with Mustard and tried to forget about the throbbing foot.
They knew they would need to pack away soon, but they risked a longer stay and tried hiding themselves ever so slightly in the plant life, they were sly, and this was not the first time even with one of them limping. Even as grown adults they had hide n' seek down to an art form.
The Park rangers could not see them, they were well hidden and once they knew they were safe they put all their stuff back and put their tents up.
'Just like when were lads...nice n' easy!'
They spent hours chatting, laughing, eating, and drinking and were by the end pissed.
They sat unaware to their surroundings in a state of intoxicated bliss amongst their cans and wrappers delighted in what they felt was nothing less than heaven.
They were unfortunately unaware as to how vulnerable they had

become; they had left a chaotic platter of snacks for wildlife to feast upon and they were so unsuspecting in their beer fuelled state that they were now offering themselves upon a platter.
There is nothing quite as delightful to a predator than the perfect hunt, to rip flesh from the bone of a squealing defenceless life.
'Miccel..Muck..Mick..can you s..shee..dat?' he pointed a shaky drunken finger to the other side of the lake to two beady red eyes that watched from the bank and then another pair and then another so on and so forth, the eyes were intently glaring in their direction from the darkness.
'Kids on biks..bikes?'
'Lots of 'em if it is, eh?'
'I'll av em, fuck em right up'
He stood pretending to box but instead tripped backwards into the water much to his friend's amusement.
'Twat!'
'Mate...mate...look!'
The eyes were moving around the lake fast, they certainly were not bikes and it was also becoming clear they had seen the two from the other side.
'I think we need to go...NOW!!'
'Watcha onna bout...!'
He turned around in the water but could not see a thing, the red eyes were not there anymore.
'AHHHHHH...FFFFFFuuuuuCKKKKK!'
He spun around to see his mate with two large black dogs pulling on his arms and legs in opposite directions and then a third plunged its teeth puncturing his throat sending a spraying of blood down his chest.
'H..He..help...ME!' he cried, and wailed but his friend was frozen and backed further and further into the water as the dogs pulled his friends legs and arms so hard they ripped away and left him rolling and crying in agony as the dogs feasted on his separated limbs gnawing on his bones and tearing away layers upon layers of flesh and then ripping away at this throat, pulling away stringy pieces of

muscle and flesh that slipped away like a someone pulling apart a Lasagna.

His friend sobbed and vomited into the water trying to be quiet enough that the dogs didn't notice him, he could see one of the dogs rip away his friends clothing and then as he slowly faded away one of them bit hard on his groin tearing away in a game of 'tug of war' until the beast received it's sinew'y treat.

The dogs hunger didn't end it just grew, and their movement was hard to see for the final friend as fear and alcohol interfered enough that he couldn't tell what was real and what was a figment of his own imagination but regardless he was no longer hidden and the dogs circled him and swam at him with fierceness incomparable.

He managed to pull himself on to a small island with a tiny cluster of bushes and trees but he had no where to run and he prayed that any moment now he will awake at home, the dogs reached the island and perfect unison they pounced upon him feasting upon him until his face was skinless, his eye lids licked away and with his last breath his glistening crimson skeletal face let out a whimpering cry.

'M..m..mum!'

24 hours later

'I did a full sweep honest Officer...I checked, there was no one here...if there was, they were bloody good at hiding out the way...I..I...how do you think I felt to find that poor sod when I arrived in the morning, eh?'

'I understand your upset Mr. Scriven but every detail we have is imperative in solving this case...In my ten years of service I haven't seen anything like this, whoever...or whatever did this was utterly monstrous. We don't have wolves nor bears in the UK, and I am certain a fox would not do that...'

There was no sight nor sign of the dogs ever placing a paw on the park, no hairs nor faeces found and no trace on the body found by the bank and no one could ever figure out how...the dogs bite marks were unlike any bite mark yet Mr. Scriven's dna had been found

around the body.
Mr. Scriven was charged with first degree murder and was sentenced to life without parole, after a month in prison he took his own life leaving this note on the wall written in his own blood:

>			*GOD*
> *IT WAS NOT ME*
> *I AM NOT THE BEAST*
> *PLEASE TAKE ME SAFE*
> *I ANDREW SCRIVEN*
> *INNOC...*

His wrists were cut and with a device he had managed to quietly concoct without watchful eye, the family of the boys shared a mournful Merlot when they had heard the 'Beast of Billericay' had killed himself.
'He'll rot, the Pig...filthy fucking Pig Beast!'
Mr. Scriven was innocent, he was kind and was a devoted father and grandfather.
Mr. Scriven was a member of the model boat club, was a proud Union representative and a doting family man who had planned to take his grandchildren to see a new film in the cinema 'Harry Potter and the Philosophers Stone'.
He had been reading the Harry Potter books with his grandchildren; they devoured every page and were collectively excited.
No one attended Andrew Scriven's funeral.
His Grandchildren grew up without mention of his name ever again and were incapable of finishing any of the other books nor did they ever watch any of the films, anything that could be a reminded of the 'Beast of Billericay' was scratched away from their life.
The Beast of Billericay had no gravestone, and no one laid flowers, his wife went on to marry Walter Schrader-Smith a member of the Rotary Club and local UKCP councillor.
A year later there was a vigil for the two lads that were killed:
Michael Knowles, 31 from Basildon.

Jason Carter, 31 from Wickford.
Both had attended the same school, and Jason was a soon-to-be father, candles were held for them both and they each had their favourite songs played (Black Hole Sun by Soundgarden and All the Small Things by Blink 182.)
The entire case was rapid, and conspiracy theorists were lapping it up like flies over shit on online forums.

CODECRACK3D: It's so obvious ain't it, those boys were killed by the cops, bet they planted the evidence on that Scruven bloke.

USAPATIOT247: ARE YOU FUCKEN SIRIOS!!! CLEARLY TERROR ATTACK JUST A BIG COVER UP TO PROTECT IMMIGRUNTS!!!

Christluvzme89: I think you are right USAPATIOT247, that or those boys were just DAMNED...Sinners perhaps?

BIGRICHARD69: Dunt surprise me tho if it was that Scriven bloke bit of a loony lefty I eard..

Hammersman62: BIGRICHARD69 My dad was a union bloke he weren't "Loony"!

There were similar events with just as gruesome results, yet no one had connected the dots, a year prior four cats found severely mauled in a large Basildon Park and two years after the deaths of Mr. Carter and Mr. Knowles there was a car accident at Hanningfield Reservoir. Those that attended the accident described the way the lady's body had burst like a balloon unusual for the type of crash considering the car had no more than a small scratch, the Fire Fighters that had attended had never seen a fatality like it especially the weird markings on the skin/

Animals go missing often and the police do not go looking, the owners never stopped looking and printed posters that were placed on lampposts, fences and trees yet only rarely are the animals found. Five years after the Beast of Billericay two cows in a field in Benfleet found standing upright with their intestines in a puddle below them, it was as though a missile had blasted through them (yet how they were standing upright had still been a mystery.)

Billericay High Street - January 2021

'What's his name?'
'HER name is Jess...'
It was clear the lady did not appreciate the old man referring to her a dog as a boy but in his defence, he was partially sighted and thought the dog was a post.
'Joss?'
'No! JESS!'
'Oh, sorry love, these bloody masks, eh?'
'Yep.' she rolled her eyes.
'How old is Jess?'
'She has just turned four.'
'Well, she is a gem, bless her.... anyway, enjoy the rest of your day!'
The man moved on swiftly, yet the lady blanked him and continued walking her dog, she arrived at a coffee shop and tied Jess to a lamppost while she went to order a coffee.
'The regular I'm assuming Karen?'
'Yes, that's right and please only a smidge of cream thank you'
'No problem' *you miserable cow.*
Karen took her coffee and paid contactless tapping her card impatiently, she walked down the high-street sipping her coffee and suddenly realised she had left poor Jess tied to the lamppost and she quickly hurried back.
Jess was there, she looked confused, but Karen just gently patted her head after and they began their slow stroll to the nearest park.

The Park was large and was accessible for most, with plenty of room for families and those with dogs.

Karen had a small Tennis ball placed inside a small bag in her pocket, she had quite a nice throw and launched the ball a considerable distance and Jess launched after it at great speed until she was out of site.

Karen finished her coffee, she checked her phone for emails and her inbox was full; she worked for a housing association managing families that ranged from young parents all the way up to those that required certain levels of assistance and the wrong sort of place for someone who was filled to the brim with scorn with those she looked upon as below her, even those she worked with found her utterly repulsive and the residents found her inept and demonstrably egregious.

A couple of minutes had passed, and Jess still had not returned with the ball, Karen had barely noticed and ignorantly assumed that Jess was just distracted and so she slowly wandered to where she expected her dog to be.

She found Jess's collar by some trees; she picked it up and strolled inside until she herself was out of sight and by a tree she found the Tennis ball with a large bite taken out of it.

'Jess!!' Karen moved further inside the area, she moved aside branches and eventually she found her Dog 'JESSS!'

Her Dog was there amongst some leaves or at least what remained of Jess, the padding of her paws had been scorched away and so had both of her eyes and as Karen stood there the dogs body deflated like a soufflé and whatever was once flesh, bone and organ oozed out of the dogs mouth and anus in a disgusting bloody soup that gurgled and bubbled like it was cooking on a hot plate.

Karen backed away unable to speak any further, tears poured down her face and she attempted calling the police but her palms were so sweaty she dropped the phone; she felt disorientated and by the time she had picked up her phone night had fallen in what felt like seconds and there was no one to be seen. She looked at Jess' corpse and there was a sudden red glowing like car headlights and moments later a dozen pairs of eyes had surrounded her revealing a mass of black dogs.

There was for a moment of beautiful calm silence and then just before the dogs leapt to at her, a face became visible, and it was certainly not a dog. The face was male, had a pale complexion, green eyes and a gaunt expression and just stared vacantly at her from amongst the mass of trees and dogs.

Karen had no chance to scream as the first thing to feel teeth was her throat and as the dog let go she clasped at her throat blood gushing down her fingers, and then as she took her final breath two dogs leapt up to her arms pulling her out into a crucifix position as their claws sunk into tree trunks.

She was found in the early hours of the morning by a separate dog walker, Jess' body was no longer there, and Karen had a noose around her neck contradicting the monstrosity of what had truly killed her.

```
TheThirdEye4: Twenty years this reeks of gov
cover up as here we have another suspicious
death, sus as fuk.

RemnantsofGod666: She was last seen walking
her dog, dog now missing WTF!!!!

PatriotProud1966: People need to wake up, I
remember the Beast of Billericay always know
itwasnt him it was just obv. Scriven was a
good bloke, always said hello.
(2001 reponse - PatriotProud1966: Filthy
fucker hope he rots in hell!!)

BIGRICHARD69: Hope they find the dog.
```

Karen King was pronounced dead and there was a puzzled discussion amongst those that knew her, she was not a parent, but

her mother was still alive and although the Police said those that are suicidal may hide their pain, it really did not sit well with her family.
'My daughter didn't do that to herself...'
'I understand this must be difficult for you Mrs. King but...'
'MY DAUGHTERRR WOULD NOT HAVE DONE SUCH A THING!' she sniped back, and she never shed a tear not even once. Unlike the Beast of Billericay case the Suicide of Karen King was quickly beginning to unravel especially considering unusual markings were discovered on her body.

Part II

LINK LINK LINK LINK
LINK LINK LINK LINK
LINK LINK LINK LINK
LINK LINK LINK LINK
LINK LINK LINK LINK
LINK LINK LINK LINK
LINK LINK LINK LINK
LINK LINK LINK LINK

The Coroner sat behind a desk facing the Officer visibly stressed and exhausted.
'It's not Suicide, but what's even more puzzling is we also can't figure out how someone managed what they managed because the gash on her neck doesn't quite fit...the last time we had this kind of issue was twenty years ago...'
'The Beast of Billericay!'
'These marks on the neck they do not match any known blade nor device, there is something weird, yet they also do not match any animal bite. I have done done some digging and I have also uncovered this...'
The Coroner slid a file across the table and there were decades and decades of people and animals with what were described as "Unusual Wounds" or in some cases when recorded as murder just "N/A" was placed upon the file.
'How has this gone unnoticed for so long?'
'Mr. Pullman, I wish I could answer that question, but I feel it's only my familiarity with the two poor souls in the Beast of Billericay case that have drawn to this conclusion...'

RemnantsofGod666: BASILDON VOICE WERE FORCED TO RETRACT THEIR ARTICLE ON KAREN KING'S DEATH!!

BillericayDave1958: My neighbour said the field was completely foggy night of her death, streets seemed fine. FREAKY.

TheThirdEye4: Pics of Beast of Billericay case leaked online, gave me nightmares BUT shit those wounds are weird. No sign of Karen King's death pics but would not surprise me now if wounds are similar. Those that investigated the Beast of Billericay are being pulled back out to investigate

this case and others.

United4Life: Yeh okay...

TheThirdEye4: Can't say how I know but mark my words a) this site gets taken down and b) they find links between other cases, remember what happened to those cows?

Police were found darted all around Essex investigating cases some of which were sixty years old all of which were filed incorrectly and then just left, dismissed, or forgotten.
'Those tin foil hat fuckers have been on our case again mate' an officer said as he lent against a fence.
'Always are, they write so much bullshit eventually something sticks.'
The police were investigating the obliteration of two cows in 2006, the farmer was more than happy to speak to the police
'Well, ya see, I remember coming out and they were standing there and I just...froze. It wasn't simply that the cows were gone because in that first moment I don't think I thought that what I was seeing was real, they still moved a little at first and one of them was still chewing grass but their intestines, heart and stomach's were in a puddle of blood and muck below em'...their eyes..their eyes were gone as well...'
'What then happened?'
'I phoned you guys and well...it went so far, made the paper at least but it went no further, and me and my late brother Chris ended up burying the poor sods over there...'
'Would you be offended if along with a coroner...we dig them up?'
'Well, no but won't they be you know pretty non-existent by now?'
'That is very possible yes but If our hunch is correct, it might help solve a current case...'
The farmer did not have much else to say and he stood mesmerised by how the death of his cows would be helpful to the police and a Coroner...

Sasuke13: Didn't believe it at first but police are investigating that farm with the two cows that were obliterated.

TheThirdEye4: Getting Freaky. Fr!

ALM247: Bet they wer all terrar attax! #COVERUP

'Are we really doing this?'
'Yes mate, we are...hand me that shovel!'
It was dark and two large portable flood lights lit the ground where the farmer informed them, he had buried both cows.
'This is grim you know that right?' the officer contemplated throwing their shovel to the ground 'What are we expecting to even find?'
'Markings...'
'Markings? You really expecting to still find these markings? This really is a shot in the dark...you know this case will be closed quickly don't you'
'That's the thing...I don't think it will, you see nearly every one that has dealt with these cases left them in a state of limbo a sort of legal loophole was formed...'
The second officer had nothing else to say, they decided to continue and help the other officer began to dig for the corpses.

TheThirdEye4: GUYS! GUYS! OMG! Have you seen how many weird cases in Essex have been abandoned. They were affected due to something called 'The LINK CHARTER.'
THE CHARTER IS LIKE A MYSTERIOUS CLAUSE THAT ALLOWS A SORT OF LEGAL FREEDOM: FAST ARRESTS, IMMEDIATE CLASE CLOSURE REGARDLESS OF EVIDENCE, ANY CRIME/ INCIDENT IS OPEN TO CHARTER...NO DATE ON WHEN IT WAS CREATED BUT

BELOW EACH OF THESE FILES IN THE BOTTOM
RIGHT CORNER THE WORD 'LINK' IS HIGHLIGHTED
IN A BOLD BLACK INK STAMP.
SOME OF THE CRIMES ARE WEIRD AND
PREDOMINANTLY IT'S JUST ANIMAL DEATH'S BUT
THERE ARE MANY OTHER CASES FROM CAR CRASHES,
SUICIDES, GAS EXPLOSIONS AND EVEN ONE CASE
OF SPONTANEOUS COMBUSTION!!!!

UNITED4LIFE: EVIDENCE?

THETHIRDEYE4: CHECK THE FILE SECTION OF
FORUM IVE CREATED FOUR FILES - CASES,
PHOTOS, INVOLVED AND OTHER.

UNITED4LIFE: Just Chcked and okay...that's
all fuckin freeky!!!

Sasuke13: Big cover up damn!

AjonesPeakyBlndr: Bullshit!

CanisCognitionis: @THETHIRDEYE4 I have sent
you a message, would like to discuss.

'Think I felt something then, what about you?'
'Yeah, something is there...we are definitely close'
It did not take much longer and there it was, they could not grasp at first what it was they had discovered, and it was becoming clear that the hunches were certainly looking more real.

'They haven't decomposed...'
'Nope' The officer gulped.

'I think...'
'THEIR STILL ALIVE!'
It should not have been possible, but they were still alive, there was no beating heart and the organs that had fallen out were no more, but the brains were still live and kicking and their bodies began twitching.
 'Paralysed under the earth for fift...fifteen years...we ain't dealing with some random killings ere' this goes beyond everything...CHRIST!' Pullman threw his shovel to the ground with a mighty thud.
'So, what now?'

Barleylands Farm, Billericay - January 2021

'Nanny, can we go feed the fluffy sheep first?' the little child was oh so eager and she skipped across the stoney path in pure delight at each fluffy animal and pretty flower that caught her eye.
'First we need to wipe that chocolate ice cream off your cheeks I think sweetie pie before one of the Goats tries to eat your chubby cheeks, ay?'
The child's grandmother wiped away the dessert from the corner of her granddaughter's mouth and they held hands as they wandered to the child's desired location.
It was a warm day and there were several families with children, the farm looked beautiful with varying flowers and other plant life decorating every path.
The little girl was transfixed by every cute-eyed little thing that cried out around her, but one thing caught her attention, a small Black Goat.
'Nanny!! Nanny!! look at that goat, they are pretty I want to feed...I want to feed it...PLEASSSEEE!!!' she shook hard on her grandmother's arm and the pair moved over to the goats.
'Okay! Okay! Come on then!'
The grandmother was not really paying much attention to the goat

and was thinking about other things, worrying about the child's poorly mother and worrying about whether she has enough money on her card to buy her granddaughter some lunch.
'Oit...Cherrrub...Come ere'!' a nasty voice called at the child.
'Nanny?'
'No... No... No..not Nanny! Me!'
The little girl looked closer, and the small black goat stepped towards her, she investigated the goat's jet-black eyes, and she could see a horde of growling hounds with glowing red eyes looking back at her.
'They won't hurt you little one, they just want to be friends that's all!'
'Friends? They look scary?'
'No..no, not at all they are my friends, and they are your friends!'
'Do they want to play?'
'Oh! Yes, yes, yes! They certainly do want to play with such a pretty little cherub like you'
'What game could we play?'
'Hmmm...let's play 'What is Grandma?'
'How do we play that?'
'I close my eyes and when they are closed you need to move your hand a little closer to my head until you can stroke it and when you get there, I can tell you what Grandma is!'
'Okay!'
The little girl began to slowly move her arm stopping abruptly every time the Goat's eyes opened until she finally reached the Goats head where she carefully placed her hand upon its head.
'What is Grandma?'
The Goat's eyes opened, they were a nasty and aggressive crimson.
'A BITCH!'
The Goat made a horrific snarling and foamed at the mouth, and it bit deep into the girl's arm as she cried a deafening cry, the Goat's teeth had passed through flesh and reached bone and the poor child's grandmother tried so desperately to stop the animal's clasp on her granddaughter.
'Help! Help! Please!' she screamed out to those around 'HELP!'
Several workers appeared and with great effort they managed to save

the little girl from the jaws of the Black Goat, the Grandmother was enraged and as a First Aider attended to the child she snatched a pitchfork from one of the farm hands and jumped the fence to where the Goat now cowered In the corner, she walked slowly with the pitchfork scratching at the floor below with an ear piercing scraping noise.

'Cunt!' she snapped at the Goat as she drove the Pitchfork through the skull of the Goat penetrating its brain, the Goat's eyes widened, and its tongue flopped out of its mouth with a waterfall of blood, and it thudded against the ground.

Paramedics eventually arrived and they were understandably puzzled by the situation before them, the grandmother splattered in the Goat's blood with a pitchfork in one hand and her grandchild in the other.

Christluvzme89: Child bitten by BLACK GOAT!! HELLLLOOOO! 666!! THE BEAST!!

THETHIRDEYE4: Poor thing said she could see some "Scary Black Doggies" as well, not sure if it's linked at all but cases are certainly getting stranger. Will be meeting with @CanisCognitionis to discuss some related stuff. Will keep everyone posted.

BillericayDave1958: Doubt it's all linked...bit far fetched.

THETHIRDEYE4: If that's what you believe but you could look through my files on this forum...

Basildon University Hospital Canteen
'Look at the marks of that child's bite marks and now look at the markings on the cow, they are identical and now look at the

markings on Karen King and Michael Knowles and Jason Carter...they all match!!'

'Has the case been marked Link?'

'Yep' Pullman said as he sipped his coffee 'have you seen the markings appear on any other bodies?'

'This week...four: a motorcycle accident, another suicide, a murder and... a cancer patient...'

'A CANCER PATIENT!' Pullman shouted forgetting his surroundings.

'Radiation burns and then four days later the poor sod was dead, these markings were found around their ankles, chest, legs, and eyes'

'Like eye lids?'

'No... their eyes, the eyeballs!'

STRANDED0121: I dont know if anyone else has had this experience and I could get in trouble for interaction here but I've been having these weird dreams and this forum is starting to freak me out - The first dream I had was a long while ago and I didn't think much of it but basically it involved me walking a pack of black dogs near some water nt much happened but at the end of the dream I looked into the water and there was this head looking back at me smiling. I had another dream where I was in a car accident and in the back was the dogs again and the car hit another, the person in the other car had a dogs head and was holding a gavel like a Judge...I tried getting out of the car but when I looked outside my dogs were on the other side growling and holding the door closed..and most recently I had a dream or rather nightmare where I was sleeping on a hard ground covered in hay, I remember hearing a little girls voice but then I felt something horrible like claws scratching at my brain and my eye sight was being blocked...I could hear the child screaming and when I could see again there was a pitchfork coming for my face.

AjonesPeakyBlndr: You guys are getting worse.

Part IIII. The Well

Dear God
25/01/1997
Haven't told mum and don't think Dad will believe me but I know what happened, I'm really scared and I don't know what to do.
I did not want to bunk of but I did anyway, Mr Jones is a horrid teacher anyway he always stands and watches while we change and dad won't care because they are friends and dad always defends his friends.
I shouldn't have gone though, oh my please forgive me.
It's not my fault though, is it?
I'm always very good and I always have top marks but I have never wanted this to happen, not this.
You see Tom has always been really nice, I really like him and I thought he liked me and I told him not to do it but he didn't listen to me.
We walked far too long, we walked past both sets of shops and through the small park and even that scary big one where Gina's horrid sister always waits (She wasn't there this time, guess we were too early.)
I really wanted to kiss him, I really did.
We went to this area, there was an old Well that apparently was haunted or something like that and I didn't believe it not at first.
He sat on it when we arrived and pulled me close and then there was this sound that began from the Well like a dog crying.
Tom looked inside and he said the more he leant forward the more he could hear the dog and then he reached further, I said it wasn't a good idea and that instead after school time we should ring a vets or something.
He didn't listen, why didn't he listen?
HE SLIPPED and then there was horrid noise like gurgling and growling, and then I looked down very briefly and I couldn't see him but I could see these dogs and there was loads of these big black wild dogs with red eyes and then this horrid face and it was white and pale and had these horrible green eyes.
If I call the police then what?
Please god...Please save him...Give me an answer...WHAT DO I DO?????

Kim
x

Empire Pharmacy, Wickford High Street – February 2021

She walked cautiously, she cast her eyes across the counter and there was no doubt that the Dispensing Assistant had their eyes upon her watching her every move. Her intentions were clear yet what they had not realised was that she had already slipped a pack of Phenylephrine into her handbag.
She settled on a couple of cans of deodorant and wandered to the counter, she asked the Counter Assistant for a pack of Promethazine and as she turned her back she managed to steal a pack of Pseudoephedrine, she assumed successfully but the moment she paid for her things and left the Pharmacy the Dispenser was contacting the Police.
She barely made it to the end of the the high street when then they arrived, there were only two officers, but her glazed expression was demonstrable to her arrest.
She did not resist, and she sat in the police car quietly, she just gazed out of the window watching the world pass by and she did not utter a single world.
Her eyes were sore, and it was not just the sun beaming through, as they entered Basildon she shifted uncomfortably.
"If you need the toilet, you can go when we arrive!" One of the officers said in response to her shuffling but she did not need to go, she had not visited Basildon since she was at school as she avoided it like the plague making longer journeys just to avoid it and as they passed through, she closed her eyes.
When they arrived, she kept her head down, she spent the whole time staring at her foot until she was inside and thats when she finally spoke.
'Name?'
'Kimberley Marshall...'
'Date of Birth?'
'10th of March 1985'
She was scared the whole time and the moment she noticed the officers shuffling through her bag she began to fidget, her palms

were sweaty, and it had nothing to do with the medicine that she had stolen.

The officer that wanted to speak to her was ever so eager to do so and rushed her into a room to talk and Kimberley felt as though her entire world was about to end.

'Kimberley, this is your first offence...and I can't force you to comment on what I am going to ask you but...this diary entry in your bag.'

Kimberley sobbed, as she expelled over twenty years of pain the Officer.

'Kimberley would you be willing to go with me to the Well?'

She cried more so than before, and she could not utter a word.

'Would you like a tea or coffee?'

'I WANT TO GO HOME!' she screeched at the officer.

There was a banging on the door.

'Pullman! Are you done yet?' a second officer expelled at him.

Pullman just signalled to him that he would only take a minute more and he began to whisper to Kimberley.

'Kimberley if you can help me, I might be able to solve this for you, I'll help you and we can fix all of this pain!'

Kimberley just nodded and with Pullman's help all charges dropped, he told the others he was dropping her home but that was not true. Her nerves only escalated, her stomach knotted and contorted as though riddled with sickness and as they arrived close to destination, she felt a violent rising sensation that hit its peak when the car parked and quickly stepped out to vomit into a bush.

'Better?'

'Not really, no...'

'This will all be over once you show me where it happened, chin up!'

Pullman's obsession with the case was starting to show as he was unshaven and constantly with a glassy expression like he could see something no one else could.

Kim led him through some trees and onto a cobble path that trapped inside swarm of nestled brambles, they were both caught and stung so often but they pushed on.

The Well stood before them like an ancient shrine and Pullman's eye's lit up and wandered over to look down but he could barely see the bottom, Kimberley could not look like every time she tried, she could only see that horrific memory etched deep.

Tears rolled down her eyes and Pullman had not even noticed her pain.

'Kim...Kim...I need ya help, think it's best I go down and check it out!'

'No, please...sir...Officer...DON'T!'

'Can't hide from this forever, eh?' he smiled at her 'Don't despair because we will sort this together, yeah?'

He had forgotten he had not even discussed with her, what he knew about the other cases, and he had not contemplated what he was doing to her by pushing her into the web.

Pullman had robe hidden under his shirt that was tied around his waist, and he was sore as shown by the marks now visible.

'With this end tied to my waist and the other tied to the tree, we should hopefully be able to secure me enough that I can take a look...'

Kim aided Pullman, she was slow and visibly uncomfortable.

'We do this and then I take you home, yeah?'

'Okay...' She said looking at the floor.

Pullman sat on the edge of the well and slowly lowered himself, he used the bricks and the holes of those that were missing like stairs, and he made his way down with the occasional slip due to the moist moss that plagued its walls.

Kim looked down in fear but she wanted to see just so she knew he was safe, she hoped that seeing his feet hit the floor would remove at least some of the negativity around the Well; Kim started to realise however that once Pullman reach the Well it was possible he would see Tom's corpse and she contemplated running far far away.

There was a thud as Pullman hit the muddy floor and a nasty putrid smell reach Kim's nose.

'Stinks like shit down ere'!'

Pullman crouched down and turned the flashlight on on his phone,

only to discover a small tunnel wide enough for him to crawl into.
'Kim, I've found something interesting!'
'Wh... wh...what is it?' she was dreading the answer.
'A tunnel...I think!'
He got onto his hands and knees and his hands squelched deep into the ground clawing at the filth below him and moved forward holding his phone in his mouth until he reached the end which led to a small cavern not tall enough to stand in but wide enough for three to four people to sit inside.
It was surprisingly warm, and it was clear by the bricks that surrounded it that this was never built as a well but as a hideout or for storage (to hide things from thieves.)
Pullman held his phone high around the cavern yet there was no sign of any body not even a handful of bones however there was something striking, painted across the wall were images of a dog like creatures and there were hundred of these drawings creating an army of these dogs surrounded by varying words and notes ('Shuck' and "Garm" were the most prominent names.)
He took many photos inside the cavern, and as he did so the light from the flash showed more detail that he had not noticed moments before and with each flash a sense of overwhelming foreboding hit him hard and he quickly crawled out of the small cavern as he could no longer stand the snarling horde of Dogs that all seemed to gaze into his eyes.
'KIM! I'm coming back up!'
There was silence and she was no longer looking down.
Pullman grabbed the rope and climbed back up to the top, he was tired yet increasingly concerned about Kimberley.
As he reached the top, he pulled himself over and threw himself to floor rolling as he landed.
'Kim? Help me up!'
Pullman was met with silence and as he sat up it was clear that Kim was nowhere to be seen.
'Kim? Kim?' He checked his phone once more and realised that over two hours had passed from the moment he checked the cavern.

'How? How? HOW?!'
He drove home quietly and even detoured ever so slightly in a hope that he would spot Kim but there was no sign of her, he hoped and prayed that she had made it home, but he was not so sure.
He opened the glove compartment and grabbed a CD (Metallica – The Black Album), he clicked play and turned the volume up loud enough that no one could hear him scream and cry into his steering wheel; he sobbed hard letting out everything he could away from everyone and once finished he started his car and moved drove away as nothing had happened.

AjonesPeakyBlndr: looool Gone well quiet on here now haha bet you all realise how fucking stoopid you sheeps are haha

Sasuke13: @AjonesPeakyBlndr get a life boomer.

AjonesPeakyBlndr: I have a bloody good one thanks snowflake haha

Sasuke13: Yh okay...sure.

'Daddy's home!'
Pullman's daughter was eight and in her school line she looked like one of the Hobbit's standing in the Fellowship of the Ring much smaller than the rest of her class.
'Hey there, my little princess!'
'Hobbit Princess?'
Her dad laughed and he held her close.
'Well, if you are the Hobbit princess the who am I?'
'Wizard! Daddy Gandaf!'
'Awesome!'
As he carried her into the living room his wife approached, and they embraced with a big kiss.

'Daddy! Daddy! Daddy! Can you read me a story for bedtime?'
Pullman was tired, he did not want to read her a story in that moment and just wanted to rest but he knew how much it meant to her.
'Okay but here is the deal, I'll grab three books, and you get to pick your favourite!'
'Deal!'
He took her to his bookcase, and he picked out three books: The Wizard of Oz, Northern Lights and Alice's Adventures in Wonderland, she picked the later excitedly clapping her hands with glee.
Pullman tucked her into bed, and he sat on a beanbag reading with her, the little girls' arms were wrapped around her cuddly Unicorn and she eventually drifted to sleep, she snored, and Pullman smiled enjoying the sweet faces she pulled as she drifted off into her own little Wonderland.
'I love you very much Hobbit!' he kissed her on the forehead.
He wandered downstairs and poured himself and his wife a glass of red wine.
'Something's wrong, something is really wrong...' his wife said as she stood watching him carry the glasses towards her.
'Why do you say that?'
'Wife's intuition!"
'Work has just been weird that's all...'
'Could you take some time off?'
'Im not sure I can...I want to but this case...It's complicated...' he sighed.
His wife took the glass of Wine from his hand and kissed him on the cheek.
'Go get some sleep, we can have a drink another night...'
He held her for a moment in a tight embrace.
'I love you so very much!'
Pullman then wandered to bed, he did not bother cleaning his teeth and nor did he wash instead just kicking off his trousers, taking off his shirt and then jumping into bed in his pants.

He slept for only four hours and then awoke swearing in the middle of the night where he sat up browsing the web.

```
Search: 'Essex Black Dog'

Search: 'Essex Devil Dog'

Search: 'Shuk'

Search: 'Garm'
```

He stumbled upon so many articles and many adverts for ghost hunting trips, but something did catch his eye; there was a pub in Billericay 'The Old Crow' that had so many sightings that the original owner abandoned it.

'You awake?' his wife turned to him.
'Yeah...sorry, did I wake you?'
'A bit, but it's okay. What did you find?'
'Want to go to the pub tomorrow night?'
'Together?'
'Mhmmm'
'Uhm...yeah, sure but which one?'
'How about 'The Old Crow'?'
'Never been...' she thought for a moment 'Wait...isn't that the "haunted" one?'
'Uhm...yeah, I think there are some stories...we should get a babysitter...'
'It's short notice but I guess I could ask Rebecca...'
'Awesome!'
He still could not sleep and stayed awake till the morning, his mind was engaged, and he made a large breakfast and a pot of coffee and poured some orange juice.
He was given the circumstances slightly chipper; he had a spring in his step and a smile on his face.

'Well, someone is well rested...'
'Yeah, you could say that!'
'I've sent a text to Rebecca by the way!'
'Sweet!'
They sat and enjoyed breakfast together, he gulped down two cups of coffee and a small glass of juice which washed down his bacon and pancakes.

BIGRICHARD69: Dog was never found..shame.

Sasuke13:No, the dog was never found I'm still very curious to what @THETHIRDEYE4 has discussed with @CanisCognitionis.

Pullman's morning went so well right up until he had a call from work, he left the room to take it and when he returned his spring had stopped and his head was low.

'Oh honey, what's happened?'
'I've been taken off the case, the Karen King case..."
'Why?'
'They didn't say...'
He took his little girl to school and once done he drove to Wickford, he still had the notes in his car that detailed Kimberley's home and he made his way there knowing full well that if any colleagues had caught him, he would be in serious trouble.
It had started raining and he pulled out a large black umbrella from the boot of his car and he made his way to Kimberley's flat, he pressed the doorbell only to be greeted with a large man with a tattoo of a spider under his left eye.
'So, it was you! Eh ya prick!'
before Pullman could reply the man threw a punch that knocked him back down the stairs he had just climbed, although in considerable pain it didn't stop Pullman and he staggered back to his feet and ran back to the man that had thrown the punch leaping at him only to be

stopped by Kimberley who stepped in front of him with black eyes and a swollen lip.
'Kimberley what happened to you?'
'Why did you make me go back there?!'
She slammed the door in his, he could hear her sobbing behind the door.

4 hours later

"*On cold eve one merchant did say the black dog beware he comes with a bite, with teeth so sharp and eyes so red... Black Shuck...Black Shuck...he comes to judge...Black Shuck...Black Shuck...a taste for blood!*" sung the bartender as he began his night of horrors.

'When you said let's go out for a drink, this isn't exactly what I was expecting...' Pullman's wife said as she looked at her husband puzzled.
'I'm not quite sure what I was expecting to be fair, but it definitely wasn't this!'
The bartender was dressed in a cheap halloween costume victorian inspired.
'On this night you shall hear tales that will chill you to the core, you will hear stories that will keep you awake...dare you come on this journey with me? BUT first...DRINKS!'
The evening was not particularly scary asides from the occasional cheap jump-scare from very cheesy actors dressed as Werewolves and one actor for some unknown reason dressed as a Zombie.

STRANDED0121: I had another bad dream, I could see thousands of Black Dogs running across the water like a wave about to flood the land yet it was like I was also one of the dogs, I could see people running yet they had no chance to run and hide. It felt like we owned the land and the last image I

had was a face so...innocent..a child..I
then woke up in a cold sweat.

Christluvzme89:You are either not telling
truth or you are DAMNED!!

Pullman's wife sat back in her seat sipping on the last of the drink she had through a straw making slurping sounds as she did so "Do you believe any of that stuff the barman told us all?"
'Who knows, eh? Who knows...'
'That poor lady though, they didn't need to pick her to jump out on, did they?!'
'Oh, come on, it was a bit funny, weren't it?'
they both chuckled as they sat in the car, listening to music.
'We better get back...' she paused as something took her eye
'Darling? Can you see that man?'
'Where?'
'In the bushes?'
Pullman stepped out of the car, locking his wife in as he checked.
'Anyone out there?' he called out but greeting him was an uneasy cold silence.
He was playing with fire as he had stepped out, but the company of his wife brought back the spark that had been missing and he felt a courage he hadn't felt in decades; it wasn't the courage of the fight but the courage of a husband and a father, the courage that stops you being scared of the dark.
There was a shuffling in the bushes and then he could see it, the two red beady eyes looking back at him and he felt the cold chill shoot down his back.

THETHIRDEYE4:Police Officer Neil Pullman
killed, he was working on the Karen King
case but was dismissed after he began
operating without the permission of his
superiors. A member of the public known as

Kimberely Shannon said that he forced her to help him go and search an old Well, she said he was practically delirious so she ran away, she has also stated that he used force.

In regards to his death, his wife has stated that he went to check on a man that was watching them from the bushes and his dog attacked him ripping out his throat. Neil Pullman bled to death whilst his wife watched on in horror.

This was outside The Old Crow, a pub famous for it's ghost dog sightings.WTF!!

PART IV

Canis

Wat Tyler Country Park, Pitsea, Basildon - June 2021

There were large numbers of children in the park, parents trying to keep distance yet finding it immensely difficult as they queued for copious amounts of cold cans of drink and Ice Creams.
The children were bursting with energy, they zipped and zagged like the wasps that chased after their confectionery, yet they all dropped what they were holding when they heard the scream, it was blood curdling.
The children ran back to their parents and cowered; the parents did not want to discover the screaming but the moment they noticed who screamed they all ran away.
Crowds of families buzzing to their cars, dropping their keys until finally throwing their children in.
He was pulling himself across the gravel path dragging his own entrails, it should not have been possible yet there he was the man that only ten minutes ago led many of the children on an educational nature trail around the park.
He was crying, the cry a man makes when he knows his life is over, the cry of knowing you do not get to say goodbye and the cry of abject horror.
He crawled for comfort, for someone to save him but with each inch he lost more life and behind him a bloody trail long and winding, kept alive by mystery.
Cars sped out of the car park rapidly causing a nasty collision that flipped two of the cars, then another and another until a ball of fire engulfed the skies.
From the deepest part of the woodland, they could see the red eyes and snarling teeth and even the clouds knew what was happening as a storm began to form.
'Mummy! Daddy!' a little girl screamed as she was separated in the chaos, but thankfully her parents spotted her in time so they could all hide away.
The only person that did not seem scared was an old bald man with

a pale complexion that stood back just watching, he did not smile, nor did he cry and just watched.
The man was wearing a long dark green leather trench-coat.
The dogs never came out of the woods, but their mere presence caused enough chaos they did not need to pounce, they just watched as chaos ensued.

Basildon University Hospital

'Thirty-six bodies, they all have that fucking mark on them!' the Coroner was alone for a moment, no one else knew what he knew, and he did not know where to start.
There was a new Mortician with him this week, a young girl and she was eager to start, and it was not long till even she started to notice the peculiar.
'Sir...sorry, the markings on the body are a bit weird, ent they?'
'Yeah...you are right very weird!'
'I know this isn't going to sound professional, but these aren't identifiable and certainly don't match what has just happened...'
'No, they don't...'
'So..uhm what next?'
The Coroner thought for a moment, whether exhaustion or not he decided to trust her...he did not have anyone else (not on a work level at least.)
'I need to show you something!'
He led her to a large file, and he divulged everything that he and Neil Pullman had discussed.
'I'd call bullshit but how can I?' she was visibly shaken 'a cancer patient as well?'
'I remember hearing for years about a Black Dog that was occasionally spotted, and I knew about The Old Crow, but this shit stretches further than that, I've traced back hundreds of years and It seems to go even further than that to old, old shit...'
'Like what?'
'A book...'

'A book?'

'Yeah, I could not find the books name but it's rumoured that a handful of pages were removed and enchanted or cursed or whatever. Over history they were used for different purposes and then this rumour went about over time...I wasn't able to tell Neil this, but I wanted to compare notes with someone else first. One page was used by a horrid man, a vile and sadistic bastard whose arrogance overwhelmed his intelligence, and he played with tools that he could not handle, and he opened a doorway to somewhere...or at least made the situation far far worse'

'You don't mean physical do you...'

'Whatever he opened was the gateway to something that felt itself important enough to be Judge, Jury and Executioner, something that could blend into the world with ease and infect every crack, crevice and corner...'

'How many cases are there?'

'Hundreds of thousands...maybe more, this isn't merely a pub that's haunted by this entity nor is it a town but the whole of Essex, every single inch like a great big Chess Board for it to play on!'

'Is there a pattern to follow or a type of person that gets pulled in?'

'The only common thread is the markings left but excluding that, no there is nothing...'

```
THETHIRDEYE4: This hasn't just suddenly got
worse, it's always been like this! It's as
though Essex just works differently, perhaps
it's best to say that every week a large
proportion of crimes and 'accidents' are
linked.

AjonesPeakyBlndr: ughhhhhh!! @THETHIRDEYE4
you need ya fucking head tested or do you
just luv the attention?!!!!!
```

There was quiet for a while, a period where there was little death and

a moment of calm as though all in Essex had gone still for a week.
There were only a handful of car accidents.
There were no murders.
No one was bitten nor maimed by animal.
No one died of Cancer.
There was not a single random home accident.
There was a feeling of thriving and prosperity, a feeling of ease had settled and rested.
The Coroner was still mulling over the incident at Wat Tyler Park and he examined every detail and every note taken.
This makes no sense he thought to himself, he sat alone in silence for an hour or two until he decided to pay a visit to the Morgue where many of the bodies from the incident were still resting.
It was at first a moment of contemplation but then he decided.
He walked over one draw where a body rested and pulled it out, he did the same to every drawer that held a body from the Wat Tyler incident until they were all out there before him.
There must be a pattern!
In frustration he decided to push every draw shut and walk away yet someone called to him, their voice was cold and rough.
'Hello?' he spun around.
There was a body now laying on the autopsy table, they wore a green leather trench-coat.
The Coroner did not wish to approach the body and continued to try and leave but the door slammed shut on him.
'This isn't funny!'
He turned around to see every draw he had opened previously reopened and there was movement under the sheets from the bodies that were soon to be laid to rest.
The Coroner turned again trying to open the door but no avail and he turned back round to see the body on the table sit upright.
The room had become icy, and he could see his own breath in the air, he closed his eyes for a moment and once he reopened them, he looked straight into eyes of the body that had sat up and two green eyes looked straight back. The figure was wearing a green trench-

coat and unaware to the Coroner this was the face in the crowd during the Wat Tyler Incident, this was the face that looked directly into Karen King's eyes and was the face that lurked around every suspicious incident yet only those that died were even greeted with the face, until now.

The figure's trench-coat was partially open, and The Coroner could see its green tinted skin, it was wounded and still bleeding; the bodies in the drawers shuffled and with a nasty growling and snarling the dogs with red eyes appeared from under the blankets with the carcass hat lay before no more.

'What in Christ's name are you?'

The figure looked at The Coroner and slowly raised its right arm and opened its hand to reveal stinging nettles and then opened their right hand to reveal crushed Holly; both hands were visibly sore with cuts and raised bumps.

'Choose!' the figure demanded.

The Coroner panicked and selected the hand that held the Holly.

'So, it shall be...' as it spoke the Dogs were no longer snarling and they sunk back down and the drawers of the Morgue closed shut 'in exactly one month, when the sun is away from the sky you will have the gift and opportunity to strike me down. You must come to where I rest, come to where I lay my head and if you succeed, I hand you, my throne.'

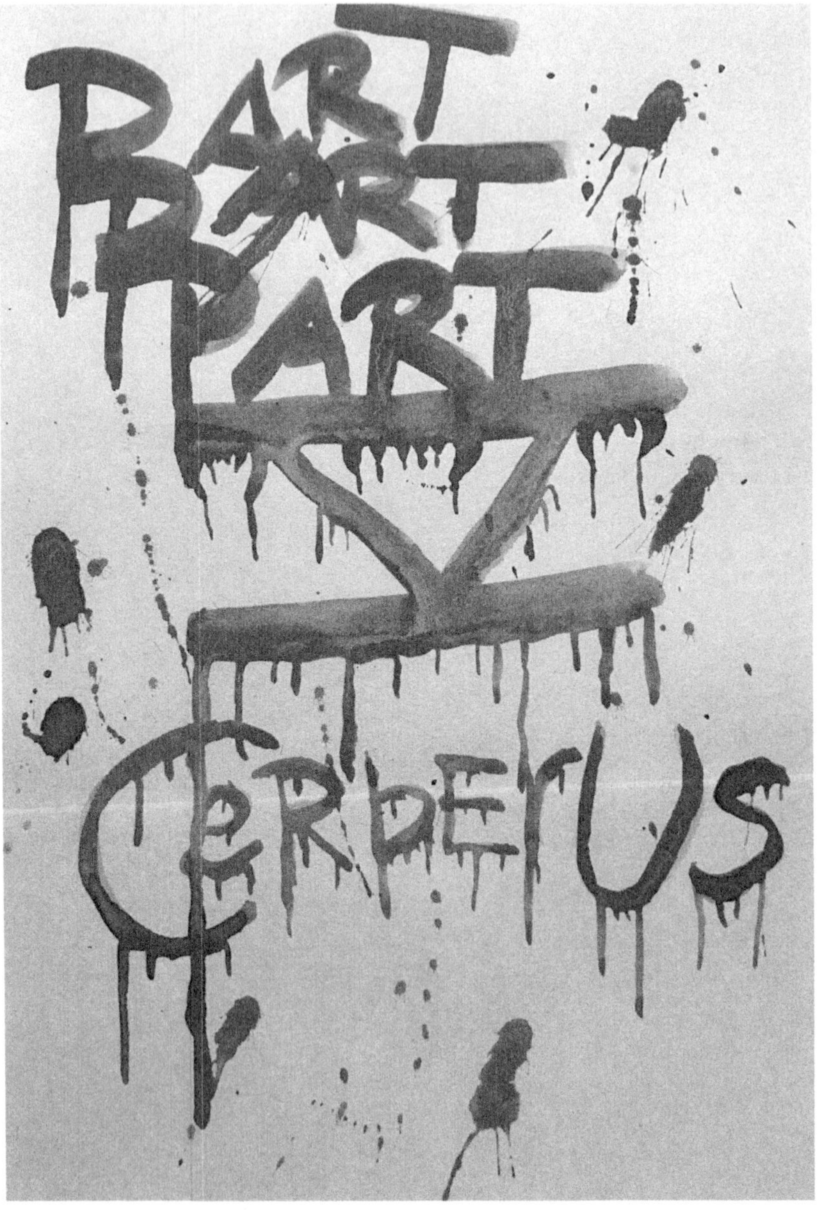

Basildon Upper Academy, Basildon – June 2021

'My brother reckons this whole Essex haunting thing is all shit...'
'Why? Have you seen all the stuff on it?'
'huh...well...yeah' he lied 'It's obviously fake!'
'Even that lady with the rope around her neck?'
'Easy to fake, my brother...'
'Let me guess your brother is an expert of film or some shit like that?' the other boy interrupted 'How many times do we have any conversation where your brother is suddenly the expert, ay?'
'Piss off!'
'Exactly, it's all shit you come out with!'
'No, it ain't!'
'It is! Remember last year?' he took a bite of his lunch and continued with a mouthful of his cheese sandwich 'all this big shit about how your brother was so skilled he could not become a Marine, that the Army feared him? Its all BS!'
There was not a s response, the boy just run off to hide and that was the fourth of fifth time in the last couple of weeks that he did that.
 Don't say shit bout my brother was what he wanted to shout but he couldn't because then they would know about Billy, they would know the truth and they would call him *Mental, Freak,* or *Dangerous* or something like that.
His brother didn't trust anyone and he believed that he had to protect his lil bro the best way he could and when he felt he was losing control he'd cut and he would do it hard and deep like it wasn't even hurting him and he didn't mean for his lil bro to see it that one time, he didn't want him to see the lamp fly across the room and he didn't want him to see the piece of glass pierce his skin..but he did.
Mr. Smith went looking for him and so did Mr. Benson, they looked under and behind everything they could until they found him, he had parked himself so perfectly within a bush it was a miracle they had

seen him at all.

'Come on Jake, lets go in!'

'No...'

'You ain't in trouble, honest! Scouts honour!'

Jake turned and looked at the teachers, they could see he had been crying.

'You can't sit out ere' alone mate!'

'I haven't been alone though...'

'Eh? No?'

Both Smith and Benson sat on the grass with Jake, they knew all about his troubles at home and it would not be fair to berate him when the kids were having rough at home as well.

'Well...who else has been here?'

'Mr. Link!'

'Is that the art teacher?'

'There isn't a teacher in the school called Mr. Link, is there Jake?'

'No.'

'Jake...what did Mr. Link look like?'

'Big green leather jacket, like really long and he looked really old, and he had big green eyes...said he would set his dogs on Sam for me...'

The teachers looked at each other with concern, they were not sure how real this Mr. Link was, but they knew either way that Jake needed some support.

Jake spent the rest of day with Mr. Smith, he was given a cup of hot chocolate and Jake just sat quietly reading a slightly warn copy of a Wrinkle in Time.

'Not long now Jake and it'll be home time, unless you want to go home now?'

'No. I'm okay...well actually...could I go just a little earlier than everyone else?'

'That's fine, we shall contact your mum.'

Jake just smiled back.

Truthfully, the school had been in contact with his parents for a while, keeping an eye on him and worried he might go down the same sad road as his brother Billy.

The Police had been notified yet no one had been able to find a Mr. Link nor had even recognised a Mr. Link that was until they spoke to Sam.
'Yeah, I did see Jake speaking to a man, but I didn't think anything of it, just thought it might have been that brother he is always on about.'
He escorted sam away abruptly, Mr. Benson took him home in his own car and the police were notified that Mr. Link had been spotted by another student and it was the student that the threat was made about.
Sam lived ten minutes away by car, but it took longer due to an accident, Mr. Benson thought it would be worth while to use a shortcut.
There was a winding road near a small woodland area and the trees all stood at a haunting angle.
'Would be creepy to be here at night!' Sam said to his teacher.
'I make you right there Sam.'
they only got halfway down the country road when Mr. Benson stopped abruptly, a large black dog was standing in the middle of the road looking at them with its teeth bared.
'Get out the way you stupid dog!' Benson screeched and tooted his car, yet the dog did not flinch yet instead it barked louder and louder, two more dogs approached and stood so close to the other it looked as though one dog with three heads.
Mr. Benson rolled down his window and leant out to make a loud noise to deter the dog.
'Move! Dickhead!' he exclaimed forgetting for a moment he had a student in his car, the dogs did not move and just continued to grow and bare their teeth.
'Fuck this...sorry Sam, shouldn't have heard me say that'
'That's okay...'
'I'm gonna reverse and go the other way, ain't gonna wait for them to move...'
Benson turned around but to his horror another three dogs appeared behind him or at least he assumed it was three dogs, he had not

noticed that the first three had merged into a singular entity and so had the one behind.

From both directions the dogs began to move into his direction, and he panicked.

'Run the dogs over!' Sam demanded.

'I can't...I can't...shhiiitt!'

The dogs moved faster until they pounced so fast, eyes an intense crimson.

'WINDOW!' Sam cried.

But they were too slow and the first three headed dog ripped onto Benson's arm pulling him through the window and he hit the ground hard.

'AHHHHHHH SAM! SAM!' the teacher cried.

The pair of three headed dogs pulled Benson near the front of the car and they began to feast on him, they ripped him bare and he tried to get away but his right arm was dangling almost torn completely away with chunks of flesh dropping to the ground as he attempted to fight for his life as he cried in desperation to save his own life but it didn't work and he tripped smacking his skull against the pot hole ridden road causing a large gash.

Sam cried unable to make noise and frozen in glittery mess as he witnessed his teacher being devoured by the monstrous dogs fully aware they could come for him next, as the dogs bit into Benson's stomach and began pulling his entrails out like a string of sausages, Sam attempted creeping out and even managed to reach for Benson's phone.

Sam managed to open the car door silently and he tiptoed towards where he could see houses beyond the trees, he wept as quietly as he could and with the lack of noise from Benson, he knew his teacher was dead but did not want to admit it.

Sam reached halfway into the trees until he became aware he was being watched; at the corner of his eyes, he could see red dots moving around but he did not want to turn and only wished to keep moving forward completely. He was being toyed with, he was remarkably close but a least thirty of the dogs were closer and they stalked him, they stalked him until the last moment.

```
AjonesPeakyBlndr: that poor fuckin kid,
don't exploit this one for the stupid
conspiracy please lets allow the parents to
morn.
They had to check the kids dental records,
there were bits of him everywhere and some
poor soul on 999 heard it all happen poor
fucker. R.I.P. Sam Parker and Alex Benson.
```

The Coroner had to look at the findings, at the horrific remnants and as he expected the obscure markings were once again there but this time something strange had happened, the gross chunks of that poor boy's body laid out into an arrow pointing back towards the school. All cases were still being marked 'Link' and nothing ever reached a court case no matter how severe. The Coroner had told no one about what happened in the morgue, yet it felt horrifically clear that this poor boy's body had wad used as decoration and a nasty clue, he wanted to tell everyone that he knows who did it (or what did it.) yet alas he could not.
Jake's mental health deteriorated after the incident and he was found by another student in a dire state, his hands were bloody, and he just looked up with a blank stare.
'I... I... didn...didn't...th...think he...w... w... would actually d... die...'
he then cried a cry that echoed across the school, it was loud and caused teachers and students alike to flood to poor Jake.
After that day he did not return to the school, no one knew what had happened to him, but it was clear he would not be returning and there were so many rumours floating around.
'Bet it was his brother that killed Sam and Benson, it's obvious innit? His brother's mental!'
The students were as always cruel.

PART XI
WEB

The Coroner took a pile of files home, no one questioned the stack of boxes he had taken home in-fact no one ever mentioned what he was doing not even the Mortician.
The files were piled high, they were colour coded, detailed, and intricately marked.
His drive home across Broadmayne felt tedious as he found himself caught in usual rush just after 17:00pm and his stop the local shop to grab a large can of Red Bull, his mind was scattered and he didn't even realise he had forgotten his mask and card until he shamefully got to the counter and handed over a £2 coin to a displeased lady on the counter.
His heart was racing even prior to his first sip of the energy drink and he knew he was in for a night of high anxiety followed by truly little sleep.
His house was immaculate and the moment you stepped in a took a single glance at his Marble kitchen and stunning living-room where everything was white or cream and there was for those that wandered inside an overwhelming attack of their nose with Lavender.
He had taken every box and folder he had collected to his spare room and removed three cork boards that he had ordered days prior from the attic.
He had removed every file from the decade he was born and had organised them chronologically and it was this meticulous planing that led to his discovery.
There was no doubt that a pattern was standing before him and as he placed a series of photos from the 70's on the corner of the chalk board, he began to see it.
It's a map? A fucking map!
He rummaged through his cupboard to find an old map of Basildon and another of Billericay, he stapled the two together and began drawing over them the patterns he was seeing to reveal a series of tunnels that all led to below Great Chalvedon Hall public house – it was no secret that the public house dated back 500 years but this was more extensive than that and revealed a network of tunnels that

seemed like giant termites were living below every home but The Coroner knew it was considerably far worse.

In a small notebook he had Pullman's notes, and he found the sketch he had made of The Well and made note of it on his map, everything was piecing together, and he knew it stretched further afield than just these two towns.

He went to his computer to do some digging after he added every marking from the photos to his maps and he began to investigate the that haunting figure that visited him, he felt certain it was this Mr. Link that had also visited that boy but the term Mr. Link seemed to only appear a handful of times and 'Link' only via Link cases.

Search: 'GREEN MAN?'

Search: 'MR. LINK'

Search: 'GREEN MAN AND BLACK DOGS'

Search: 'Basildon Dog Well'

Search: 'Chalvedon Hall Black Dogs'

The list of searches was vast and there was nothing overly striking at first and it all seemed hopeless...

No witnesses or at least he thought at first and it wasn't until a spelling error lead him to Sir Gawain and the Green Knight that he began to spread further a field and he began researching the West Midlands for similar stories, there was nothing recent no sign of any unusual happenings but it became clear that perhaps at some point the haunting covered a wider land as there were crimes and incidents that seemed quite odd such as soldiers missing on patrols only to found decapitated not long after in completely abandoned areas or animals being slaughtered beyond what would have seemed possible. The Coroner never usually felt ill during his work but this moment was different as the amalgamation of graphic images and the intensity of his white walls drove him into a depressing spiral for five hours where he swirled in and out of brutal nightmares that splashed his mind in a wall of blood, a wall of blood that had been dominating his every waking hour.

When the morning arrived, he found himself still in the room surrounded by his nights work and realised that Mr. Link's message was soon approaching, and he was certain that no action would result in himself becoming a part of this Macabre web of location and death.

His heart raced all day, he did not eat, and he had occasional sudden bursts of tears he stomach rolled around in horrid anticipation of his own mortal decision, but he knew that with what he now knew that he had no other choice but to face off against the green man.

He phoned his parents; he phoned his sister, and he wrote a resignation letter to his job.

'I'm just going away for a while, it's all to do with my job thats all…could be weeks but maybe longer…' he didn't know what would happen but he tried to clear space so no one else got caught up in what he was about to do 'Yeah I love you too mum..' he took a long sigh and tried holding back any tears 'and you Dad, I love you too..'

He rummaged his shed and brought out the toughest items he could and settled on a combination of three - an Axe, Shovel and Pitchfork. He constructed a holster for the axe which he aimed to carry on his hip. He filled his car with all sorts of other equipment from various forms of strong tape, ropes, a torch, and a visor to protect his eyes and then he just prayed he would not meet any Police.

He spent a while sitting in his car, his heart fluttered, and he felt a feeling of loneliness he had never felt before infused with a horrid feeling of dread that clawed at his mind.

The Coroner's old anxieties were returning, and he felt like he was drowning.

I CAN'T…I CAN'T…I can't do this! Why…This isn't fair…it isn't fair, not at all…WHY ME!

He had eventually fallen asleep against the steering wheel, nightmares ravaged him, and he felt every horror he had experienced overwhelm him from his ex-partners unexpected announcement she was going to leave him, the house fire when he was a child and finally Mr. Link and those horrid dogs.

He would not have normally fallen a sleep in the car, but it was clear he was exhausted, and it would have been useless to even attempt fighting it.

```
THETHIRDEYE4: It's all gone quiet, nothing
new not no big cases or anything.

Sasuke13: You say that like it's a bad
thing!

THETHIRDEYE4: No it's not a bad thing, it
just seems well...strange, so much chaos and
puzzles then all of a sudden absolutely
nothing.
```

The Coroner awoke himself with a spluttering cough and with a shudder tried sitting up only to suddenly place his hands over his eyes as the morning sun strikes his eyes, he pulled out his phone to check the time and a cold sweat hit him like a brick.
10:00am How the fuck have I managed that!
He started his engine and drove to the nearest Takeaway and ordered a hefty breakfast, orange juice and coffee, he devoured the food and guzzled both the coffee and juice and just gazed out of the window watching passers by just live, some laughed and some refused to make eye contact but he took it all in as though it was the last chance he would have to do this.
He spent the day hovering around town, visiting locations that he could picture on the map aware of the labyrinth that lay beneath his feet and as he did, so he felt his very own black dog approaching.
I can't do this, I really can't...I just want this all to end.
His palms were clammy, and his heart raced, he wanted out and he

did not want to move any further only wishing to stay here out of sight; his stomach was cramping intensely, and he could not tell if he wanted to be sick or cry or both.
Please, please let this nightmare end.
He could see Mr. Link's cold dead face repeatedly in his mind.
NoT lOnG nOw, Eh?
The Coroner for a moment closed his eyes and pictured somewhere beautiful, he pictured a holiday in Greece and he pictured the crystal waters and the sun burning his cheeks, he pretended he could hear children giggling and splashing in the waters but it was to no avail as he could see the red eyes rising from the waters and out charged an army of snarling black dogs with Mr. Link strolling forward behind them.
Everybody on the beach was ripped to shreds before his eyes, there was so much screaming and crying yet he could not open his eyes no matter how hard he tried until he felt that tight clasp around his face of four meaty fingers and a thumb squeezing his cheeks tight together.
'Ya wallet and ya car keys now Prick!' said a rough looking twenty something year old in a rugged green tracksuit, he held out a small knife to the Coroners belly.
'Ay...eh, don't try anything silly, eh? Look just one moment, my wallet is in my...my jacket ov..over there!' he pointed to a large rock that was resting besides a bush, the thug strolled over and as his back was turned the Coroner cautiously lent down to pick up a different rock that was the size of his fist and crept behind the youth and then with a violent swing of his arm he cracked him round the back of the skull, he stumbled at first and then fell to the ground with the Coroner unaware whether he had killed them or not, he didn't care.
The Coroner jumped into his car and he drove to Chalvedon Hall, he was cold and numb with one singular intention; he drove as fast as he could with little care for the other cars on the road.
Once he arrived at the hall he just sat there and contemplated what he was going to do, where he would start and how he would do so. He sat in the car for hours; his hands were tight on the steering

wheel gripping with anticipation for what was ahead of him.
I do not think I can do it.

Part VII — Mice

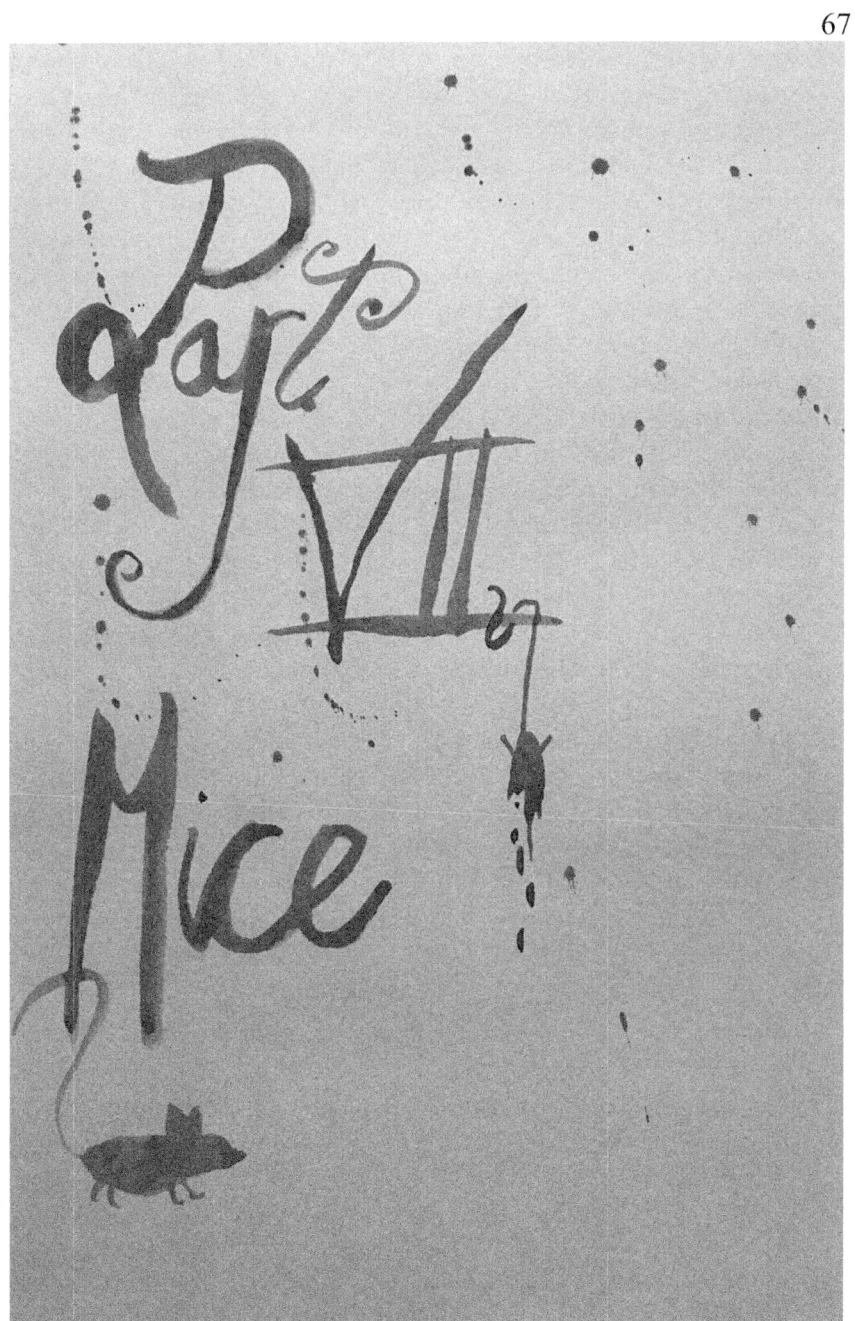

It's easy to fall, it's so very easy to allow that which stands in our way to force us to retreat and give up; that all consuming job thats eating our lives or perhaps its the loss of someone we love thats drowning our hope or even the negative figures in ones bank account a week before payday. We feel the fog approach and the dark cloud tempt us to hide, to stay silent and refuse to offer word in the moment of our depression; Shout, scream and cry in anger or fear but don't turn your back, not for one moment because there will always be someone waiting to hold your hand through the dark. Nothing is perfect but in the same breath nothing is truly hopeless.

The Coroner had waited a mighty while in own contemplation but his waiting was over and there was no waking soul to bother him this night, he pulled out his altered map and searched for the hidden entrance and he was truly glad he had brought his axe of which he had just reattached with his custom belt.

There was a tree round the back of Chalvedon Hall and it was not as it seemed, as the Coroner approached the tree, he could see the dogs faces scratched into the bark and he knew that this was where he had to start.

It was getting darker and had become surprisingly cold, he felt a cold chill slither down his spine and as he stepped back, he gasped in pain and suddenly threw his right shoe off in panic.

He felt queasy looking at his foot but there was no denying what it was, it made no sense either but there it was a nettle buried under the nail on his big toe oozing with blood; the pain he was subjected to was indescribable and he felt himself go weak at the knees.

WHAT THE FUCK was what he wanted to scream but instead silent tears just streamed down his face like a waterfall and he tried to push on limping as moved, he pushed aside bushes and weeds until he found a smaller Well similar to one Pullman visited and thankfully although completely overrun with plant life it wasn't as deep.

The Coroner sat on the edge for a moment, still in agony but nudged himself off the edge and he fell like a sack of coal on the bottom with an awkward thud and his landing was surprisingly more comfortable than he had predicted.

It was gloomy and dark with the only light that broke through was via the foliage that was webbing the well.
This is grim The Well had a putrid smell and it was clear that a waste pipe had leaked into it, he had to crawl forward but it was extremely difficult for him not to gag even slightly, there was a sudden drop as the path dipped at an angle like a slide and he slid into a putrid pit. He was succumbed by a fresh pain, and he opened his hand to see Nettles stuck between his index and middle fingers making it difficult to grasp the torch he had scrambled to find.
Some people are evil but they are evil in a way only they can and the more arrogant and self righteous they are then the worse they become; they always deliver news or messages like a judge sentencing you to death as keepers of Morality but truly they hold no true care for anything other than their bloated ego.
It was the horrors of humanity that had constructed this labyrinth under Essex, this overwhelming maze felt as though it was created by very clever termites and The Coroner was about to meet the Queen.
Scratches danced across the walls in a ballet of pain, it was a clear sign The Coroner was not the first soul to have ventured down here but he was the first for an extraordinarily long while.
His pain had increased, and new nettles had appeared stuck to his armpits and on the inside of his thighs rubbing against his groin, he was struggling to walk any further.
He fell to his knees and began to crawl the rest of the way, he found a better pace on his hands on knees but it wasn't perfect as the putrid mud that caked the floor was filled with broken pieces of nettle and thorns from other plant life and he was almost certain there were things crawling between his fingers.
The maze was opening further, but he found himself stuck with the choice of two separate paths, one sent a cold breeze whilst the other was releasing a smell of undeniable death and decay.
He crawled towards the cold breeze; he looked down to see Centipedes crawling around the mud and it made him shiver and almost freeze where he had knelt but instead persisted on until he

entered the next route where he was struck with a bitter cold.
His head felt heavy, and his eyes were feeling sore as did his fingertips, he knew what it was and let out a painful sigh as he tried moving forward but he could feel the nettles under his fingernails.
He crawled the equivalent of ten steps further until he could not take the sensation in his fingers any longer, he sat down and with the axe he kept on his belt and in aguish pondered whilst he glared at his fingernails and the nettles that were beneath them.
The mud was colder here, it was ice cold and the deeper into the mud he placed his fingers the colder it became until his fingertips were numb.
He placed the blade of the axe underneath the little finger on his left hand and writhed away until with a gasp of pain he ripped the nail away, he sat for a moment his mind swirling and trying to adjust to the pain he was experiencing.
He could not handle treating the others and he knew he could not be this reckless again as he now had to contend with this wound, he felt faint and once again he had slowed considerably.
His hand was in agony, and he could not put pressure on it and instead tried putting the pressure on his arm causing him to lean at an angle.
His eyes were terribly sore, and he kept trying to take moments to rest them, but it did truly little, and it only added to how faint he had become.
Once again, he could hear Mr. Link breathing inside his head, it was louder and more intense, and he could hear how gruff his voice was. The moment the breathing stopped he could no longer open his eyes as Nettles were now under his eyelids.
'Threee bliiiind miiiice. Threee bliiiind miiiice. Seee howww theyyy runn. Seee howw theyyy runnn. Theyyy alll runnn after the farmer'sss wife whoooo cuttt offf theirrr talesss withhh a carvingg knifeee, diddd youuu everrr seee such a sighttt in yourrr life, AS THREEE BLINDDD MICEEE!' Mr. Link's voice was no longer in The Coroners head but echoing the nursery rhyme throughout the cave on repeat, his voice was loud and penetrating like nails down a

chalkboard.

With his eyes shut tight and in pain he was becoming subjected to an onslaught of nightmares as he crawled across the ground, the army of dogs were infesting his mind with horrible visions of them ripping people to shreds.

The Coroner crawled without idea of where he was, the ground was moving downhill, and he had no idea he was approaching a hole in the ground that was a similar width and depth to the Well.

It only took the equivalent of four steps and he fell hard to the bottom with an appalling crack, he thought he landed on a twig but that wasn't the case at all and he only realised as he attempted to crawl forward but was unable to move ahead as a new pain take over his whole body and fell face first into the mud. He reached around to his Left arm only to discover one of his bones poking out through his skin and more nettles that were ravaging his body.

He became unconscious and from the shadows four beady red eyes stalked over to his body biting down on his trousers and dragging him away.

Two Days Later
Basildon Academy – July 2021

'Told ya! His brother was mental!'
'How can you be so sure it was his brother?'
'Obvious innit?!'
'Poor Jake...feel bad for how I... I mean we treate- '
'You really feel bad for that freaky family? They ad it comin to em'!'
'They were butchered, the lot of them...Christ I mean, you know it's bad when for a family of four there was ten bags removed containing body parts...'

THETHIRDEYE4:Not sure if recent killings are connected but all contacts I have had regarding this whole situation have gone AWOL.

Wasn't just that family though but also one of the teachers, a Mr. Smith who was found a day later in a burnt out car and im not sure if this is connected but a young lady called Rebecca was also found dead, her body was found in an alleyway and another lady called Kimberely was found decapitated in some woods near house...

AjonesPeakyBlndr: @THETHIRDEYE4 I think we should be more concerned bout you #FREAK.

THETHIRDEYE4: What are you trying to say?

AjonesPeakyBlndr: You just seem to know a lot about all this stuff, a little too much. Think you should be reported to the police.

//@THETHIRDEYE4 has left the forum¥¥

The school children piled into the hall winding around chairs like they were in a maze, they eventually sat nervously and quietly waiting for the head teacher's decision.
There were police standing in four corners of the hall seeing like hawks and the students that had picked on Jake were waiting like prisoners by observing the guillotine.
The headteacher strode into the hall her head hung low, and her eyes filled with tears that she quickly tried to wipe away.
'In my career in teaching I have seen some awful things, I have had to sit in meetings that broke my heart, and I have had to make decisions that kept me awake at night. When I entered this job as silly as it might seem to many of you, but I wanted this school to be a safe place, I wanted it to be a haven for those that might not always have access to such. Schools set rules all the time and theres no doubt that kids hate them, even I don't like some rules but I promise

that no decision is ever made to hurt anyone nor make anyone sad nor angry, I have had to make a decision this time under the supervision of the Police, the council and Social Services that breaks my heart and I know for many it will seem a good thing but this school is no longer safe-'

She could not continue what she was going to say and she burst into tears with two of the students rushing up to console her whilst a Police Constable stepped up to finish off what the Headmistress was saying.

'Each student will be given Impunity for being out of school as will your parents, the council are currently organising a system in which to support your families but from this afternoon this school will be closed whilst further investigations are made. There is no hiding the repeated tragedies we have been faced with here, these are some of the most harrowing cases we have had to face and we need to make sure you are all safe and although you will be given Impunity you shall not be allowed to wander the streets without an adult with you. Those that do not have parents or guardians meeting them or picking them up arrangements sorted to escort you home; your form tutors have been given the next steps, and we aim to have you all home before school finishes.'

PART VIII
RIGHT
WRONG

The students filled with a hybrid of emotions, each form room filled with some students crying from fear whilst others laughed gleefully at the knowledge they were going home and could just sit back and chill in front of their TV's whilst others were going to break the rules regardless.
Some teachers were walking students back home themselves; some were driving them home and so were the police in a mass effort to get the children home and given the circumstances it went well. Those that considered they would be pulled into accusation due to their bullying of Jake were so utterly relieved to not have been called out by the head teacher and police.

Basildon Police Station

A call had been made to the police in regards to the crimes and a man was brought in for questioning but it was clear after 48 hours that there was no further action needed but what they gathered from the individual was a conspiracy theorists nirvana as what they had now gathered was an intricate mapping beyond any investigation that even they had discovered, the gentleman in question was prominent on online forums usually under the name THETHIRDEYE4 and although usually stepping into the land of the absurd with his theories there was no doubt that his ability to piece together puzzles was extraordinary.
'He genuinely believed no one would be able to do anything?' the officer scrolled through the paperwork 'he has sat here with this just reaching out or at least he thought he was-'
'Do you really believe it though? All that supernatural stuff, fucking ghosts, and demons?'
'It's all the stuff Pullman was looking into, wasn't it? Look where he ended up-'
'Best not discuss that here mate, boss gets quite upset about Pullman...'
What they were unaware of was the effects of the Link case had

dispersed, the cases were free to explore and that wasn't necessarily a good thing as it opened up many a dangerous path and trap; There was an omnipresence to the haunting, a consciousness that etched its way into everything and could alter so rapidly that there was little anyone could do about it.

The Well, The Farm, Lake Meadows, The Park, Basildon Academy so on and so forth were all once again investigated but this time so thoroughly with teams of Police in a noticeably short space of time on their hands and knees in a desperate bid to end whatever this was now.

With the barriers of the haunting removed it did not take long for them to stumble upon hidden wells and burrows that gave entrance to tunnels and such with some only big enough for an animal like a dog to get through.

'Dear God, what have we uncovered?' said the Constable as he gazed at what he had just discovered.

The Coroner awoke, he rested yet still submerged in darkness unaware that Mr. Link had loosened his control, and the Police were beginning to discover what was lying beneath Essex.

Is this death? The Coroner was convinced he still could not see and refused to open his eyes in fear of the agony that might grip him but still he persisted.

He was able to open his eyes and felt a strange level of happy, it was not a hopeful happy but enough to satisfy him briefly.

It was damp and dark, and he could not see what was before him, but he progressed forwards with his arms reaching forward hoping to find something to grasp on to.

He walked for at least ten minutes; he had not noticed that all his bodies pains reduced although he had noticed his movements altered yet he could not understand why.

It was not just his bodies changes, there were other changes occurring, yet he would not have been able to explain if you asked him.

He eventually stumbled into an area, he coughed, and he could hear it echo everywhere.

'Hello?!' he shouted out but he could only hear his own voice echo outwards into the distance, he wandered forward for a further two minutes until he stumbled into an object before him and then hew was greeted with a choir of fire that illuminated in rings around him, there were nine layers with each at a height above the previous but all circling The Coroner.

It was a Colosseum, a nasty black circular pit that held the object that he had just stumbled into – a large Holly covered throne stood as a haunting obsidian dominating the centre.

He looked at the throne and from certain angles he could see Mr. Link sleeping, but as he moved around curiously Mr. Link was no longer in the seat yet reconstituted with kaleidoscopic scattering moments later fractured only briefly. An illusion distorted depending on perspective l

There was a loneliness and an emptiness, and The Coroner had not yet contemplated looking at himself to see why there was little pain even though there was an increasing curious fear.

He stepped backwards and turned away from the throne and began a staggered pace around whatever this place was, there were corkscrewing columns that twisted upon every level.

There was minimal light entering and it only broke through a stunning piece of art that decorated the ceiling a mighty 100ft above where he stood, it was a mass painting 50ft either side and displayed a now warn depiction of the army of black dogs.

The eyes in the painting were distinct and The Coroner could not gaze at them for long because every time he did, he could hear them, each dog was running and snarling yet still held motionless in the painting running through swarms of nettles and holly.

The police were still wrestling with their discoveries trying ever so hard to push on unaware of what was ahead of them, one officer a young lad called Collin tripped so elegantly yet landed so abruptly and with horrific consequences; Collin coughed up two handfuls of blood and died so quickly, he had landed on a large rusty hidden piece of steel girder that was out of sight.

The Constable had to move tons of rubble to access his discovery yet the officers that were with him were not lucky because the moment they removed the rubble something clasped at their ankles and pulled them inside.

'Sam! Mike! Where did you go?'

Only screams could be heard, and they went on for so long that the route suddenly became clear to the Constable.

Christ! What the fuck was that?

Every officer excluding the Constable either died or dragged inside and brought to the exact spot the Coroner was standing.

The officers were hanging by their ankles to the ceiling of the colosseum with nettles covering their mouths, they looked like prey for a giant spider, but it was it was so much worse.

'What's going on?' The Coroner panicked yet once again Mr. Link's voice crept inside his head.

Ring-a-ring-a-rosies, a pocket full of posies, a tissue, a tissue, we all fall down...

The moment Mr. Link's voice stopped The Coroner looked above and could see the dogs leaving their painting, they pounced upon the police officers that were wrapped in the nettles and dropped down to the floor with a painful snapping sound as legs broke followed by intense screams.

One of the officers looked at The Coroner and his eyes widened gripped by intense fear, and it was in that moment that the Coroner looked at his own arms and hands.

Nettles covered every inch, yet he could not tell, it was as though they were a part of him and then he looked at his legs and discovered that it was every inch excluding his eyes and mouth.

His eyes and mouth textured like nettles and had little venomous spines around them, he reached for his tools, but everything was gone.

'What have you done to me?' he screamed at the throne, but Mr. Link was no longer seated there.

'We HaVe MaDe YoU iMmOrTaL jUsT aS YoU cHoSe!' one of the dogs said to The Coroner.

'I did not choose for this! I wanted to end this!

'YoU pIcKeD tHe HoLlY!'

Mr. Link suddenly appeared before The Coroner as if carried to him by the wind, he opened his large green coat to reveal a a torso of rotting flesh and bone with centipedes crawling around his rib cage and nettles nestled where his organs should be. He grabbed at the Coroner's hands and pulled them inside making him grab at what was at the centre – a repulsive beating heart, it was riddled with maggots and released a putrid smell that caused The Coroner to heave.

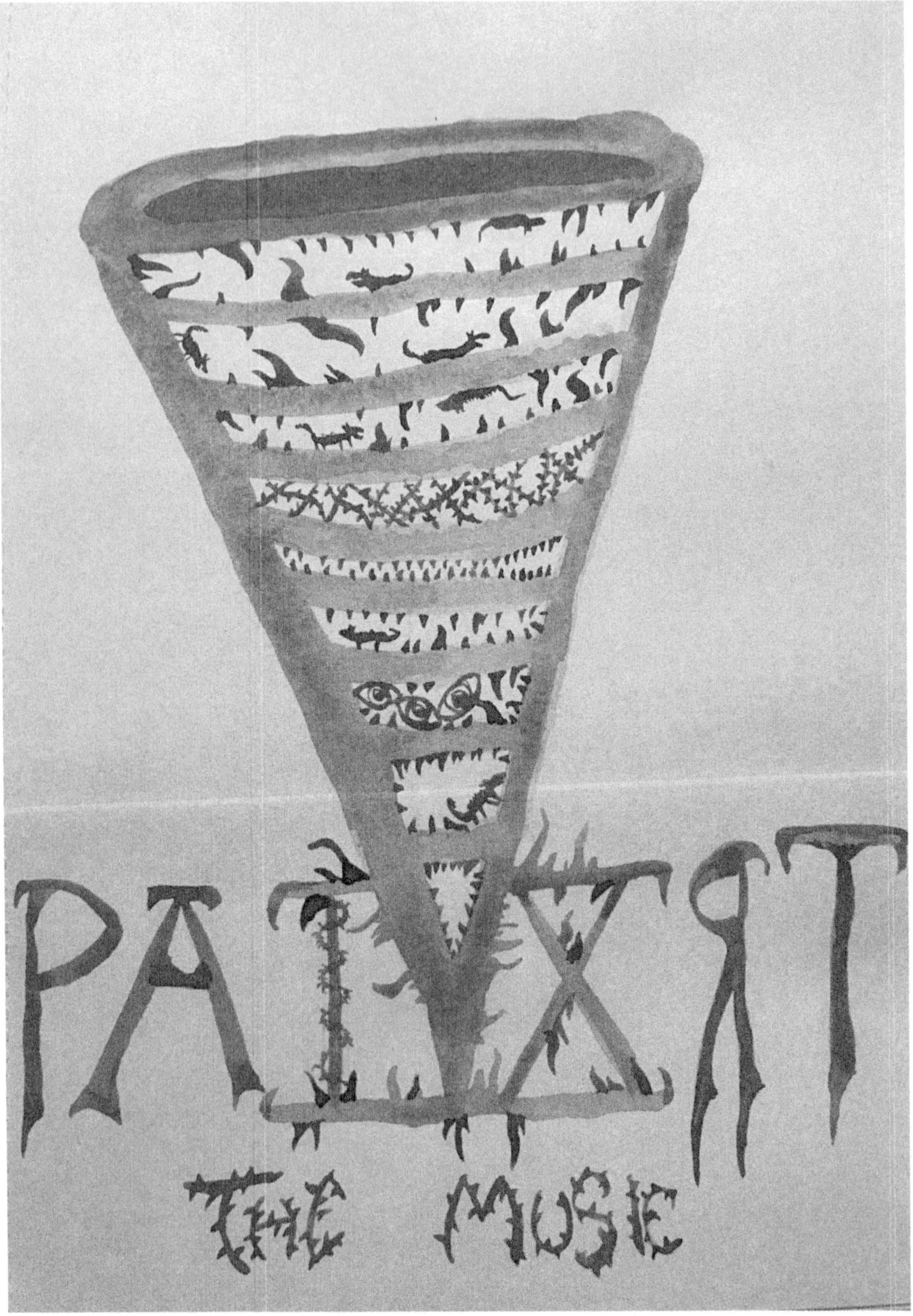
THE MUSE

The Constable had begun venturing inside the Labyrinth that his officers were dragged into, he had little care about how reckless his actions were and just staggered onwards following a small line of blood from one of his officers who had been cut on their way inside; the path the Constable had taken was narrow and winding and he could see quite clearly the anguish his officers must have had to endure. He eventually found himself on his hands and knees crawling through a narrow tunnel, he moved forwards but struggled under the intense cold breeze that was whistling towards him.
Sweet Dreams he heard a voice say and then within seconds a rumbling followed, and the tunnel collapsed trapping him inside unaware which way he was facing, unable to move and with only a small gap supplying air to him.
The Coroner was still holding Mr. Link's wretched heart in his hands feeling it ooze between his fingers.
'You said I can strike you down and take your throne...what did that even mean?'
'The moment you picked the Holly it started, my freedom!' Mr. Link sighed for moment before turning to the dogs 'FEAST!'
The dogs began to feast upon the officers, ripping through the nettles that had encased them and pulling out their intestines like spaghetti whilst another bit into and burst an officer's stomach like a balloon.
The cries in pain were nightmarish and once they had finished devouring the corpses they revealed they left one officer still alive, she was delirious and shivering in terror.
'Get the fuck away from me!' he cried.
Mr. Link snatched the heart from The Coroner's hands and forced it down an officer's throat with his fist, the Officer fell to floor and Mr. Link vanished.
The Constable was still alive, he was strong, and he began moving so vigorously he had discovered he was not as trapped as he first assumed, and he managed to free himself from the mud falling forward trying to catch his breath and then moving at a faster pace than he had previously.

There were even more things crawling around the ground, the earth was pulling the Constable a little tougher as though it was trying to imitate quicksand.
The dogs grew in number multiplying at a rate that overwhelmed The Coroner and they darted into the hard seats that surrounded all nine levels circling The Coroner, they all barked fiercely causing him to jump repeatedly. He was a wreck.

One thousand years prior– Date unknown.

The conditions were harsh but the cavern was safe and only so much sea water ever breached it, there was something peculiar and his journeys across the lands brought much rebellion and destruction and stories echoed across towns that led him to exile.
He was a beast to some and a hero to others but there was no doubt that there was something strange about him and deep down in the back of his mind he knew what it was.
It was there in forests this thing; it was different and a life without a body craving to live but he had no idea how vengeful this thing really was.
When he slept, he could see it at the corner of his eyes with mighty antlers and eyes of a bloody red watching him as he slept, it tried telling him its name, but he did not understand the words it spoke. He would forget it was there sometimes but over time they garnered a language, it was elegant yet jarring but it was most certainly effective, and it became clear why vengeance was on its tongue.
It did not like people, it found them callous and wretched like wasps. It was powerful and fierce, he did not know where it came from, but he was not sure he could now live without it.
The cavern grew and grew until it consumed entire towns with a system of intertwining tunnels. The mortal man and divine entity over time linked together becoming a soul being, it's thoughts became his and vice versa and they stalked and played with the most repugnant of humanity by luring them into the cavern to slaughter and devour, they even flayed many a man and woman that entered

that cave and used the skin to decorate it's entrance, so many lives and so easily swiped away from the world.

With each life they took, a new life would be born until dozens become an army of hundreds and then over time thousands, they stood as one but bound by three entities of mortality, divinity and the reborn.

The lives taken became haunting black dogs with those beady blood red eyes and they were the third part in the evolution and were aptly named "the Orchestra"- this roaring and drooling army of dogs that together brought a symphony of blood and destruction to those that so unfortunately stepped in its path or became prey.

The mortal man became the Link between two vastly different realities.

The name Mr. Link was merely accidental and came in from the early Victorian era, the whispers of the man in the shadows and the bodies that fell into the clutches of a being so indescribable, centuries of slaughter brought new techniques and methods like children strategising their games until exquisite perfection. Mr. Link and his Orchestra had death down to an art form and they could toy so effortlessly with feeling and reality that they lost all sense of why and became so passionate about the hunt.

Mr. Link was not the only figure however, there had been others throughout history, but none were as devoted nor as successful and the divine being favoured Mr. Link like a parent that favoured a particular child.

The number of lives truly incorporated into the Orchestra was unknown but there was no doubt that if pushed slightly it would not take much for a decision to rampage and consume entire towns or to drive people into destroying themselves.

The Orchestra had collected nurses, teachers, children, police, knights, bakers, prostitutes, priests, doctors, pharmacists, retail workers, the sick, the homeless and with each life came knowledge opening secrets, pathways and even who to target next.

Was the Coroner special? Not by anything remarkably obvious, if anything at all it would be that there was no single link other than his fascination with the case and it was this blank slate of a man that was so tantalising for Mr. Link and the Orchestra, the Coroner was the perfect specimen for the forth step in their evolution.

Mr. Link's hand was still inside the Officer's throat ensuring that the Officer was unable to resist, once Mr. Link was satisfied he forced two of the dogs held them still and then he wandered into him in a sight that could only be described as steam in reverse.

'I thought I am supposed to strike you down?'

There was silence, there was no answer, but the officer's once motionless body turned their head towards him and smiled, the room and every pathway submerged in total darkness neither the coroner nor the Constable could see.

'Shit!' The Constable exclaimed, he reached for the walls and tried to feel his way around, yet his nerves had not eased as he stumbled with every other step.

The Orchestra had left the Colosseum and begun to descend upon the tunnels by scuttling across the ceiling like cockroaches.

The Coroner did not know what to do nor where to move to and just paced back and forth in the darkness, there was just him and silence, there was no sign of light nor was there any sound not even the soft noise of wind passing through.

Red dots flickered through each winding route and they were darting around the walls, floor and ceiling with an unusual snarling and panting; The Constable started to hear the increasing noise yet could see nothing and he knelt down to the floor to feel for his route unaware of the sentience in the earth that was toying with him and pushing lost objects through the sludge of mud into his path including many of the Coroners tools and also a gun that someone had tried to bury a long time ago wrapped inside a plastic bag.

'Come on Jeff! You can do this!' he mumbled to himself in desperate motivation, his fingers embedded n the mud and oozed pleasantly between his fingers, he crawled further forward completely unaware how far he truly was to his destination.

His hands gripped something, and he pulled it out, he had his suspicions, but it was hard for him to tell since the item wrapped in a

plastic bag and coated with mud.
A GUN? Really? This is perfect! he felt more confident now, he was proficient in handling a gun and he felt at ease knowing that he was completely protected from whatever lurked ahead.
True evil is born from arrogance, it is born from superiority and a reckless attitude that cannot see how one's actions might not be just. The hybrid that stood as Mr. Link and the Orchestra felt like an evolved identity; an identity so self righteous in its destructiveness that it did not see any wrong in its actions with its snarling jaws ready to snap without care nor interest in an opposition. The belief that one's ideas are the only way and that other voices are instantly beneath or wrong is not evolution, but it is the devolution and that is where the entity had fallen, and it is haunting was no more than a cancer in the cracks of Essex or a parasitic infection.
I cannn hideee underrr yourrr beddd anddd I cannnn liveee insideee yourrr headdd Mr. Link's voice teased both the Coroner and Jeff with the later being teased with a following nursery rhyme.
Humptyyy Dumptyyy sattt onnn a walll, Humptyyy Dumptyyy haddd a greattt falll. Alll the king'sss horsesss and alll theee king'sss mennn, couldn'ttt puttt humptyyy togetherrr againnn moments later the constable tripped and tumbled down a slope hitting his head against a rock with a sickening crack causing him to throw the bag containing the gun through the air, he wasn't dead but he was now unconscious unaware that he had fallen into his destination with blood dripping down his head.
'Hello? What was that?' the Coroner called out panicked.
'On the floor, to the left of you there is a small bag containing a gun pick it up' spoke Mr. Link 'Now is your chance, eh? Kill me!'
The Coroner reached and grabbed the bag and pulled out the gun, he could see the red eyes of Orchestra return to watch them.
He felt a presence brush past him chuckling and he jumped backwards in surprise firing a first shot.
'Missed me!'
He tried standing and just listening to footsteps, but he could hear nothing until there was a sudden dropping noise.
I have fallen it is best you come and end things now, I am behind you on the

ground just pick me up and hold the gun to the back of my head.
The Coroner was confused yet he checked behind him and there hidden in the darkness a body on the ground, he could tell by the the clothing worn that it was the body of a policeman, and he knew in this moment it was the body possessed by Mr. Link. He dragged the body to the centre and placed the plastic bag over their head in a hope it might reduce and the splatter, he managed to get the body on their knees, and he placed the gun to the back of their head and with a deep breath he pulled the trigger. He was not as fortunate as he hoped in reducing the splatter and was hit in the face by chunks of flesh and blood with some reaching his lips, the sound of the gun pierced his ear with an excruciating pain like a hot needle.
He felt no different; he felt no connection to the Orchestra, and it suddenly dawned on him what had just happened as light began breaking through illuminating the room.
He reached down to slip away the plastic bag to see who was there only to realise he had killed the wrong person as he looked upon Jeff's face, he had killed the Constable and not Mr. Link.
He panicked and continued to clutch the gun in his hand.
'What the fuck is this?'
The Orchestra howled in unison.
He gazed at the throne and Mr. Link was seated, he was fully visible in his new body yet decorated in his familiar green coat and completely motionless. The Coroner felt exhausted, the gun was still in his hand, and he held it up at Mr. Link and tried to shoot but he was without luck as the gun was without bullets.
'What a shame, how very disappointing-'
'You tricked me!'
'We thought you were so much more; we thought you were worth the next step but how wrong we were.'
The next step? The Coroner did not understand what Mr. Link meant but he was far too nervous to even question what was next.
'What would have happened if I hadn't picked the Holly?'
A cold breeze stung him, and he was standing again with the choice, he felt conscious and capable of deciding fully aware of what would

be if he picked the Nettles. He was looking at Mr. Link who was in their original body and the Orchestra were there once again in the drawers of the morgue.

The Coroner was conscious, he felt capable of making a new decision and reached for the Nettles, the next thing he knew he was seeing Mr. Link fade backwards as the black cloud of the Orchestra pounce upon him. He could feel the grasp of their jaws on his throat and the pain of his death, he then felt nothing asides from a floating feeling that caused him to rise above the morgue; what he was now seeing was time passed and the Mortician working alone.

No!

The room grew a sickly stench, and he could not tell if the icy cold feeling belonged to his own impending death or the room, but he suddenly could see Mr. Link creep behind the Mortician to offer the same choices that he was given. He could not put her through what he was, and he begged to be returned to his original choice. Mr. Link looked up at him with a smile and the next thing the Coroner knew was a disorientating sense of spinning and falling...he opened his eyes and Mr. Link was looking back at him, he was in the Officers body again.

'There's no way out of this-' he fell to his knees sobbing 'I'm alone!'

'Alone? Look at what you can have!'

The Coroner turned to see the whole Orchestra, thousands upon thousands of dogs looking back at him their eyes glowing warmly, he could see remnants of items scattered around the ground and he began to wander around examining everything whilst Mr. Link just watched him.

He could see a large blade slightly hurried in the earth and he wandered over to it without care whether Mr. Link could see what he was doing but he moved forward regardless.

Last Chance.

Mr. Link knew what he was doing.

The Coroner clasped at the large knife and pulled it out like Arthur claiming Excalibur and he spun around ready to strike Mr. Link, in the same moment he had spun around Mr. Link was standing before him aggressively and he grasped at his mouth and began to try and forcefully regurgitate the rotten heart down his throat.

The Coroner tried wrestling with him but it was almost impossible, in this body Mr. Link was strong and capable of physically harming anyone leaving only one singular choice left as the Coroner managed to swing the blade into Mr. Link's neck over and over again.

The Orchestra growled and snarled yet they never joined the fight and just awaited to see what the outcome was. The heart was now exactly halfway between the Coroner and Mr. Link and the blade was halfway through beheading Mr. Link as it hacked deeper and deeper into his neck spraying a black blood like fluid all over the Coroner with a putrid stench overwhelming his senses.

Bye bye.

The Coroner screeched as he tried pushing with his tongue against the heart that was being forced down his gullet but with a final blow he swung the blade hard and made tore away Mr. Link's head from his body holding it high into the air to show the Orchestra until he collapsed next to Mr. Link's headless body.

Unconscious he could see a swirling universe of growling and hissing and he could see every distinct entity that was the Orchestra and Mr. Link, they were all drifting towards a throne where an ominous being that loomed over them all watched with intimidating Antlers that twisted and contorted like branches on a Willow tree. It had eyes that looked through your years absorbing everything you are and everything you knew. The Coroner was floating , he felt a pain like no other but he began to feel a pleasure that was far greater and all consuming; he was happy to drift towards this being, this god without any care as what he was experiencing was greater than sex, greater than life and more brutal than death. Embedded in his mind whispers of where he now was flickered through him *The Black Space.* 'Take me!' he spoke as felt himself reach closer and closer towards the entity 'I am yours, truly without question. What I was, what I can be and what I shall be. I am yours, eternally.'

He drifted further until he finally found himself seated on the lap of the being, he was cold yet comfortable rested for the most perfect sleep and he could sense the millions of other lives watching him and witnessing whatever this was.

There was a language that made no sense, and he could not yet tell what the words meant but the other lives knew, they nodded in agreement and as they cheered, they become the Orchestra and began barking.

Eventually the words began to make sense and drifted through his ears like soft silk, the language was indescribable, but it was without a doubt the greatest pleasure to hear and was more wonderful than his own language ever was to his ears as though this was truly The Language, the language of all.

The beast placed him on the palm of their hand and held them as high as they could just so he could see the masses and the power that they all were together until finally bringing him back down.

One we become. Ba'al.

The entity its large mouth and placed him on its tongue and slowly closed it is mouth like castle doors closing and he suddenly felt himself drift down the being's gullet.

Everything went dark, he had never seen so much darkness and when everything became light again, he was seated in Mr. Link's throne with the whole of the Orchestra around him, they howled loudly, and he felt that raw energy of what he now was and what he now served.

A new heartbeat in his chest and he connected to a hive of millions of lives and there were so many more yet to join the Orchestra to play the beautiful music.

Basildon police station was reduced to so few officers, they had lost so much and there was no trace of where the officers had even gone. There was no echo of a case and many a family mourned their lost, so many lives swept away and now all traces wiped away like a clean slate and fresh hunting ground for the Dogs of Essex.

The purpose was only clear to the Coroner even if the purpose was new, the purpose was merely just the next step in the evolution.

Basildon Academy eventually reopened after the six-week holiday and there was no mention of any incident, if any student even drew

close to uttering a single word, they were swept out of class at once with a quick word from their head of year or the head of school. There was a lengthy period of quiet that lasted days, weeks, and months but the moment everyone felt at ease and the moment everyone was comfortable that was when the Orchestra began to stalk again. No front-door was ever truly locked enough, no window was ever truly shut, no bedroom was every truly safe and no fence was high enough. A lonely walk home past the bushes and you might not see the Coroner hiding within the Nettles, a sunny day mowing your lawn and you will not even notice the Dog watching from the corner.
The Orchestra never ends, their music howls into every night and beckons like sirens in the night. With each life taken an expansion, the use of logic inferior and that meant that the chatting was getting louder. More people were noticing, the police could not hold it.
This was not one or two people going missing this was children vanishing from their beds, it was Grandad going to water his plants only for the hose to drop leaving nothing but a blood splatter against the fence and a single ear in the flowerbed.
Each school had at the very least three missing students, supermarkets had fewer staff filling the shelves and hospitals had less Doctors, nurses and no more room for any bodies in the morgue.
When the bough breaks the cradle will fall, and down will come baby, cradle, and all.
It spread past Basildon, Thurrock and was passing Dagenham.
So many going about their lives unaware they are being watched, unaware that as they cycle down the road the Orchestra are two steps away ready to pounce or as they stroll through the dimly lit underpass The Coroner might be waiting to greet them at the other end.

Scotland Yard, London – October 2022

'You are kidding right?' the officer said as he finished reading the document he had been handed.

'If only I was, but there are loads like this or at least similar-'
'So, what, we are now covering "X-FILES" ...we ain't trained in the fucking paranormal are we. Counter terrorism I get but not the bloody occult!'
'We don't know what it is, but this particular piece is the most interesting as we can't find an actual case that matches what happens but there are striking points'
'Where was it found?'
'It was found in Essex, Basildon to be precise. They were overrun with case after case of crimes, suicides, car accidents so on and so forth but for some reason to a couple of Officers this thing stood out. Weird thing though is the Station had no evidence of any of this, it was all found in some Coroners home. Look at this file here it's from this bloke who left this with his suicide note, the handwriting in both were slightly different but they believe both were written by him...'
'This reads like a horror story; it reads like fiction. You sure this bloke wasn't just writing some book; he was struggling with reality or summin like that-'
'You might be right, but the markings found on his body led him to be included in what have been coined Link cases...'

PART X

the Piper

I write to you with a tale, a truth and a fear descending into the depths of the beyond where the unsettled never rest, I could go to a deep and disturbing origin but my friends I do not know the full origin, I have seen and read enough to perhaps allow yourselves to come to some form of understandable conclusion.

My tale begins many years ago to a bitter winter air where the sting of snow clutched at my innocence and my path glistened with black ice. I held my mothers hand as usual fearful of where I shall end up, school was the typical answer for my confused adolescent self that wished to be home enjoying some form of visual entertainment perhaps watching the many delights that a Ray Harryhausen classic could bring as the visuals of nasty little skeletons came to life in front of my fresh eyes, sadly it had to rest in my skull as a dream until the clock strikes upon my chance to exit and reunite with my mothers hand.

I arrived at the gate it was tall and green; it had mud stains at the bottom where other children had kicked it, perhaps in refusal to enter the wretched building which stood next to an old church. I wanted the church to collapse... I didn't like it and soon I was going to hate it.

My mother waved goodbye and I dragged my feet to the classroom, my head teacher was nice yet a strange old man with a thick Glaswegian accent and a face like a frozen bin bag covered in thick hair whereas my teacher, a wrinkled old witch with a love for classical music, particularly Wagner. I myself admire Wagners work but not as much as she did, she had a picture of him on her desk, a picture of him on the wall and for the life of me I swear I once saw a tattoo of him on her arm but perhaps my imagination runs away with me there.

That day we discussed Charles Dickens who for a class of six year old children was a little too heavy and we were only just about adjusting to Roald Dahl yet here we were attempting to analyse and discuss the themes of Little Dorrit which was a pointless task as most of the class were more interested in what was going on outside near the schools out house which had a large chimney that seemed as though it had not been

in use since the day Little Dorrit was being published.
The beginning of what made the day distinct was that on my first break where I sat in the classroom book in hand as usual and with my little bottle of milk accompanying me , I was completely oblivious to what I was reading until I noticed my towns name flicker up in a section of the book which was titled 'Black Easter'.
The book was called 'Pied Piper: a history of Child abduction'.
What was it doing in the classroom? At the time I had not a single clue as my adolescence had not reached that sense of logic just yet. I have never seen this book in print anywhere else, and bookshop I have visited has ever heard of it.
Black Easter was my towns darkest day and it began nearly two hundred years earlier, the town was a hub of strict and quite morbid Catholicism, the Town was fascinated by Spain's Holy Week and the use of that creepy face covering (The horrid face covering garment adopted by the Klu Klux Klan) known as the Capirote which would induce nightmares into any a man's soul but for my town it only brought joy as they invited a man known as Padre Carmesi (Crimson Father.)
Carmesi wore his Capirote with joy and was not once seen with it away from his skull, it was red, taller and more distinct then any recorded it seemed to never move as though screwed to his head. Around his neck he wore a pendant which featured a cross with a vile that was presumed to contain blood, and this is where the rumours began to spread.
The story was that he captured children for his god, and that after a killing he would collect a vile of blood in honour of the Virgin mother. He thought that all children were born sinners and that the removal of one or two every now and then was his duty.
Carmesi was caught trying to murder a child whom he hid under his red robes and tried to slice their throat with his 'Madre' knife, the child tried pushing Carmesi away resulting in the Padre tripping and catching his robes on a candle yet refused to remove his robes. He went down to his knees and suffered the burns until death consumed his last

pathetic breath.
I spent the following days pondering Black Easter. I was too young to truly understand the story and it brought me such terror that was sliding down with an icy slither like a snake travelling down my spine preparing to greet me with its fangs.
I brought up the day to my family and no one had a clue what I was talking about and excluding that book, there was no reference anywhere else.
I began to have visits from Carmesí in my dreams I could picture him burning, except in my visions he was only wearing the Capirote and his chest was bare, I could see the flesh peeling away into the shadows. He let out a scream that sounded like a nail being dragged down a black board with a relentless vigour, he was looking right at me, his eyes as crimson as his robes like jewels upon a starry night. Padre began hovering in a state of meditation and with a flash he was flying at me with a scream that could shatter glass, my heart was raced. I awoke, my bed was soaked and my soul crawling to the corner of whatever shell was lurking in this dank state of life. A noise I'll never forget however was the vicious snarling of dogs that faded the moment my eyes opened.
My schoolwork was now impossible, the dream was flashing inside my mind every second I felt my presence graced with his, I could see him, I could smell his breath it stank of rotting meat and the stench was crawling into my nostrils. I could hear him call me and I needed an escape.
My voice needed to be heard I asked my teacher about this monster, she dismissed me "fairy tale's!" she snapped with a look of disgust that crushed me like a bug, I wanted to ask her why the book was in her class but she seemed overly unstable to question and I feared her almost as much as that nightmare.
School became and arduous task, my young mind could hold no more, and I just began staring out of the window, watching the trees sway in the crisp winter wind. My skin was cold, and I could not hold the pen upon which I tried to write with.
My vision became blurry and in the distance a figure

formed, a naked body with not a single hair growing in the distance, their head was stretching, and they were crying out. No one else in my class seemed to notice yet I was frozen and fixated. With my eyes I saw new nightmares begin as a Capirote was forming from this elasticated face, it was haunting the very grounds that I spent many a day kicking a ball. From the back of the field, I remember seeing a mass of distinct red eyes forming in the shadows of the bushes that lined the fences, yet I snapped out of what I was seeing when I suddenly jumped out my skin as a loud voice sprung out behind me.
"Did you hear about the Red Monk!" spoke the class clown who stood on a table during our break time, we would have gone outside but a suspicious storm grew masking the town under a black cloud.
They were all telling the tale of the Padre that was so far from what was in that dreaded book yet horrifying to know that there was a version of it still lurking in conversation.
Our teacher was angry at every mention of the tale of Padre, I was having less night terrors but more paranoia about my teacher and what was her distaste towards the tale, why did she have such a book in a class full of children?
My mother was concerned about how I was now; she had no idea about what I had dreamt and what I was seeing but she wanted to speak to my teacher as even she could see a change.
I remember my mother speaking to my teacher, the scary old lady turned into a doting old grandmother who you would expect to see making a Victoria Sponge.
 She simply said "He is a lovely boy, currently we are doing some reading. I think he is getting himself into a little bit of a muddle the poor cherub" my mother believed the lies of the old Witch, but I was silent during the whole event as the shock consumed me.
While my mother and my teacher spoke, I wandered the classroom, I did not look out of the window in fear my visions may return but I just graced the bookshelves hurrying past the one that I dread and running my fingers across their lifeless spines. Suddenly my fingers crawled upon a door nob, it was the cupboard. I had never visited the cupboard it had

been forbidden from all of us. I slowly twisted the handle, I checked to see if both my mother and teacher were distracted, and they were in some form of nonsensical chitter chatter, so I continued twisting the handle and too my surprise it unlocked.
I slipped inside the cupboard and was engulfed in shadows I shuffled around trying to find a light switch, I eventually found a chord of which I pulled slowly as not to cause a stir. My hands were sweating, and I began to pull when suddenly the door swung open and standing there was my mother who along with me shocked to discover what rested behind me, it was peculiar. There was an old wooden table and resting upon it was a pile of textbooks rotting. I had not processed it at first but across the walls were rough sketches of dogs, hundreds upon hundreds of dogs with beady red eyes but I presumed this was the mischievous activity of one of the students.
"Oh, dear you have found my little secret" we jumped, it was my teacher "The classes old workbooks, I find it hard to throw away such hard work I know I should give them back to the class, but I find it so hard."
I was expecting to find a dead cat or something but no just a pile of boring old textbooks. I was fearful of my next school day, what was my teacher going to think of me bursting into her cupboard.
The day started fairly normal and my mother asked me to apologise to my teacher but she was absent so instead we had a supply teacher, she a very pretty lady (Perhaps my first true crush) with ocean blue eyes, black hair in a fish tale and thick black eye liner which highlighted her eyes perfectly (She was around twenty five? Maybe.)
She was a much more pleasant than my actual teacher whose hair was always in a tight bun, and she had old round glasses, I would not have been surprised if I had found a broom lurking about somewhere.
The day went beautifully, I felt liberated and for once I had not even a smidge of fear in my bones. Our supply teacher even went outside with us during our break and was joining in with some of the fun and games but after break everything took a turn for the bizarre.

We all sat at our desks writing stories, she wanted to see how creative we were and as we began scribbling our ideas down on paper she was sipping at her coffee and writing. We were in a state of tranquil silence when suddenly there was a strange, muffled rumble and our supply darted to the toilets, a disgusting smell filled the air and the whole class confused I wandered over to her desk and noticed in the bin were two packs of laxatives. At the time I had no idea what they were and thought nothing of the name until one day it struck me, the one particular behaviour I noticed with the teacher was that she left her coffee to cool on our break which means someone had spiked her coffee and over time I have pieced the bizarre puzzle together.
While our supply was in the toilets, the door to the classroom swung open and in strolled our teacher (the wicked witch) who snapped "My apologies for being late but well you know...where is the supply?" one of our class raised their hands and mumbled "she is in the toilets!"
We could hear sobbing from in the toilets the supply was embarrassed and very unwell, a paramedic was called after the head teacher grew suspicious and shocked to find the supply in a horrifying state, she was rushed to the hospital and never seen again. It was not just laxatives that had been placed into the coffee.
I found the whole event shocking and felt embarrassed for the supply, and I missed her, the days after were quite terrifying. Our teacher's eyes were constantly twitching, and she kept making strange noises as though she kept hurting herself, little yelps would spring from her mouth.
When around the other teachers she was fine but when teaching she was violently unstable, it was as though when in our presence she was a malevolent being.
I wanted to visit the cupboard again, but I had no idea when the best time would be, there was something bizarre centred around that cupboard and I needed to find out what was truly lurking inside that cold and damp little room.
My decision shocked me but I had conjured a plan that could land me in a whole heap of trouble, what may surprise you is that I did indeed have friends of whom became confused with my sudden distancing but I did not want to

frighten them,, why would anyone wish to break the hearts of their dearest and when a child your closest friends are your fellowship. I confided in my friends my dilemma, the crawling terror of the Padre and the insanity of my teacher, they found my tale of woe both exciting and terrifying they also wished to visit the cupboard with me, and we agreed that there was only one way to enter the cave of terrors.
We conjured a tales to our parents that we were having a sleepover at a friends (In hindsight how cliché, right?) and weaved a spider web that could have ever so easily been unravelled, instead of going home after school we hid in the old toilets that was out by the school a strong brick block that looked like remnants of World War 2.
We waited for darkness to dance across the skies with a thousand crystals gracing its arrival and a silver sphere that was locked into position to haunt every man, woman, and child. We climbed out of the toilet's windows, one of my friends cut his leg against a piece of jagged glass and he tried to not cry out in pain. I gave him my scarf. Luckily, the cut was not deep but for our young minds it was a mighty war wound that would be etched into a tapestry.
We were crouching most of the way, we crawled through windows and fell onto red carpeted floors where odd bits of crayon greeted us with a rainbow handshake marking our faces like the lost boys of Neverland.
We stood in a room but this was not our room, the lights were off and it was an icy cold so we huddled together and I led them out of the room I was holding my mothers heavy torch which she hid under her bed, I now assume as both a weapon and just in case of a power cut.
We followed the long and winding carpet that led us through a maze of classrooms each just as boring as the next each. One of the boys began shaking and as he could see something that we could not, he was pale and was refusing to move.
  "The W… w.. window" I turned my head, and I could not see anything, yet my friend was now crying.
  "Stop please stop-" he passed out smashing his head against the ground, he began convulsing he spat blood everywhere his voice crackled and droned.

"dios necesita sangre" (God needs blood) he mumbled, the Padre was here.
My friends blood dripped from his mouth and was somehow sucked into the carpet, we all grabbed our friend and rushed to the door which led a long balcony that was over the hall. Before the balcony was a door that had stairs leading to the hall and we knew that we must try and get to the hall to take our friend to safety.
As he headed towards the stairs, we heard a strange scratching coming from the end of the balcony it was my teacher she was crawling across the floor like a dog and speaking undecipherable gibberish to herself and we slowly backed away. The friend who had been possessed by the Padre turned his head to the room and he managed a scream that could wake the dead.
We turned around standing there was a translucent figure in red robes topped of with the nightmare that was the capirote. We could hear the voice of the Padre echo across the hall "dios necesita sangre!"
We darted for the door and managed to reach the fire exit, we fled across the field and managed to squeeze from one side of the gate to the other gently passing our friend who had been possessed from one to another, we fled to the nearest building which was the church.
To run to the church was a stupid decision but we thought that no one would dare harm us in a Church, I was so succumbed by fear I had forgotten the horror that led to the death of the Padre.
We were running across the road which had iced over, we were sliding about trying to hold together with as much concentrated balance as possible. The ice had a crimson glow slither across each crack, the glow was chasing us.
We jumped on to the path and the ice began to form into several shards forming the shape of the Padre with a sharp point for a Capirote, everything was our enemy. The Padre was chasing us via the elements as fast as he could. We darted to the church but our friend thatt had been possessed fell to the floor cracking his head upon the ice-covered road, the red glow approached him and then a claw shaped chunk of ice jumped out and smothered their face and fired several

shards of ice straight through his eyes puncturing his brain. Their blood was moving like jell and was forming much like the ice but this time it was far more physical. There was no Capirote at first instead just the physical image of a man until the sky began raining thick dark blood which built the Capirote for him.
The Padre began chasing us he was a blur of red, we managed to reach the door of the church before he got to us charging through the wooden barrier that was the gateway to our sanctuary, we succeeded and fell to the hard cold floor.
The Church was silent, and we spent several hours without anyone bothering us, no supernatural disturbances just a horrible silence that enhanced a cold breeze that went with us like the breath of a dying child. I turned my head and saw a disturbing collection of memories that projected themselves above the the displayed bible. The images were the memories of the Padre, and we were seeing so many horrors of a corrupted man, a disturbing being with what only seemed a love for placing a blade to the throats of poor children.
We were huddled together on the rough stone that graced the church's floor and we sat watching a performance of terror, we could see the innocent having their young blood drained from their bodies at the hands of this monster, his red silk gloves cupping their jaws as he stuck a nice into their jugular we each were crying but unable to turn away or close our eyes, the Padre was here but where we did not know. The Padre was a member of the something called the Order of the Rag; it was undoubtedly evil, but we received little in terms of what the Order was.
There was the tapping of footsteps that was haunting us, a cold breath that danced the air and a scratching upon the old pews, I lowered myself to hide and glanced underneath the pews, I was so very scarred of what might happen to the rest of us.
The noises stopped I peered across the floor and glanced at the other side of the room in a hope that I could find a quick exit and gather help, but I could not find a thing. I turned my back to glance down the aisles and crawling like a Spider towards me was the Padre no longer a figure of blood but an

apparition that was trying to flesh out into a fresh body. He was making a noise that was the hybrid sound of both a chattering and a growl, I cried aloud, and my friends hid for cover. A single tear slowly climbed down my face, and I could feel myself slowly let go of my mother's hand, I would not give up my blood. I could feel a shadowy blade upon my throat, and I made one single decision, to save my life. He was owning my soul, and I could see and hear things, I began understanding his life and my own, how he lives and how I live.

I remember the last vision I had was of a mass of big black dogs entering the Church. I remember the bright red eyes as they watched me coldly and then it all hit me.

He is an amalgamation of several forces that twist his crimson soul and leave him in the eternal fires of despair as his own curse burns him forever, a tampered spirit that possess the flesh of those that read his name. The Padre was used like a gateway, a lingering soul somewhere between here and some dark black space. He was just a tool, a soul collector for some other force and the remnants of whatever was left was clinging on to whatever it could. Once he owns you your only escape are the words from pen to paper or finger to keyboard as a passage. Once read he reaches out....my friend is that I am very truly sorry, but I must rid of this weight like Atlas carrying the earth and pass you a new guest, a new voice.

You must be brave and plead for mercy because if you give in you will become corrupt, the same fate that fell upon my teacher, she planted the book of her own writing in our class and left an offering of names in her damp classroom cupboard.

Those notebooks were there to feed the Padre and sadly I was caught in the web, I must rid of this burden, and I am truly sorry.

Scotland Yard, London – October 2022

'Reality or not, there are always strange tales and odd coincidences weaving these cases. Images of black dogs scattered in and around unexpected places like calling cards for the most wicked thing you could imagine. It is all just some horrific cult but how does it link to Cancer patients? And that story about that bloody Padre, it is so weird, but the dogs are there. Maybe it is just a man writing a story to creep people out or there is more to it than that, but it was found in Basildon and there are so many Link cases there already-'

'So what? We are now taken on cases outside our authority?' the officer sipped their coffee with a notable sense of agitation.

'In the last few months, it has stretched outward a little bit more. There now seems to be cases in Brentwood, Romford, Thurrock...there have been cases in Dagenham, Barking and Upminster. Missing children, an increase in traffic accidents...I mean Basildon hospital's morgue is overflowing, there are specific measures in place-'

'And what? They are worried that this so-called-problem is going to bleed into the capital?'

The Officers were silent, they were not sure what they were even discussing but it was clear and obvious that they had been prepared for something never seen before.

The Link cases had evolved, it was lawless and fierce.

All officers involved could not resist discussing theories and it was not until someone mentioned the Black Dog of Newgate Prison that the theories began to explode.

'Mass Dog sightings? There have always been these stories dotted around but now it's on force and heading for the capital. If there are or have been these nightmare hounds the question is either why are they returning or what's been waiting for them? Hundreds of years ago prisoners described Newgate as literal hell and there were so many stories of a scary black dog with glowing red eyes. Could be little pockets all over...'

The Dogs of Essex did not seem to have an end goal, there was enough life born day after day and with the information gathered with each soul taken their hive although only covering one county had connected the unconnected. Ideas from the best and worst had created something far more vile than a simple crowd of barking dogs and more secrets were yet to be unlocked.

The Orchestra was making more music than it ever had, it was rhythmic.

Their song was not over.

London's Burning, London's Burning

*Fetch the engines, Fetch the engines
Fire, Fire.*

Printed in Great Britain
by Amazon